P9-DJK-331

Looking for Lucy Buick

ALSO BY RITA MURPHY

Harmony

Black Angels

Night Flying

RITA MURPHY

Looking for Lucy Buick

Delacorte Press

Published by
Delacorte Press
an imprint of
Random House Children's Books
a division of Random House, Inc.
New York

Visit us on the Web! www.randomhouse.com/teens
Educators and librarians, for a variety of teaching tools, visit us at
www.randomhouse.com/teachers

Library of Congress Cataloging-in-Publication Data

Murphy, Rita.
Looking for Lucy Buick / Rita Murphy.
p. cm.
Summary: Following the death of her favorite adoptive aunt, Lucy goes searching for her biological family, who abandoned her in an old Buick eighteen years before.
ISBN 0-385-72939-1 (trade) — ISBN 0-385-90176-3 (glb)
[1. Identity—Fiction. 2. Family—Fiction. 3. Runaways—Fiction. 4. Foundlings—Fiction. 5. Coming of age—Fiction.] I. Title.
PZ7.M9549Lo 2005
[Fic] —dc22 2004020128

The text of this book is set in 12.5-point Goudy.

Book design by Cathy Bobak

Printed in the United States of America

November 2005

10 9 8 7 6 5 4 3 2 1

BVG

For my brother, Tom,
who always knows which signs to follow

PROLOGUE

Lucretia Caterina Sandoni, heir to the Sandoni Brothers Hosiery legacy, was tragically killed in an explosion at the Sandoni factory on Mill Street late yesterday afternoon. Fire Chief Milton Sherman reported the blaze as the worst in Hamlin's history. Ms. Sandoni, 18, was believed to be alone in the factory at the time of the blaze.

I NEVER SAW THAT ARTICLE in the June 21st morning edition of the *Hamlin Herald*, but I'm sure it went something like that. I was already three hundred miles away when the morning paper landed on the front porch of our house on Connelly Street.

I was Lucretia Sandoni. But I was not dead. In fact, the day Lucretia Sandoni died is the day I began to live my life in earnest.

I go by a different name now. The name bestowed on me eighteen years ago by my great-aunt Rhodi. The name only she and I ever knew about. The name she whispered to me over the edge of my crib before I fell asleep every night so I'd never forget where I came from. "Lucy," she'd whisper. "Lucy Buick."

CHAPTER ONE

THERE WAS A RING AROUND THE MOON the night I was brought into the Sandoni clan. A bright white ring, which, according to Rhodi's tarot cards, meant a change in fortune. Good fortune or bad, it depends on who you ask. But everyone agrees that my uncle Rocco won me fair and square in a poker game down at Fumicelli's Bar and Grill on the night of June 1, 1987.

All the Sandonis were home that night with a bad case of the flu. Everyone except my uncle Rocco, who dragged himself out of bed to play in the championship tournament in Michael Fumicelli's back room. Rocco had a fever of 103 °F, but that didn't stop him from winning the championship and bringing home the grand prize.

Rocco thought he'd simply won a Buick. A classic 1968 Buick Skylark convertible—metallic blue with white vinyl interior and chrome-plated bumpers. He drove it home and parked it in the driveway so the neighbors would see it on their way to work the next morning. He put on the emergency brake and locked all the doors and went to bed. It was three a.m. All of Hamlin was asleep, but not Rhodi. She'd heard the car pull in. She'd had one of her *feelings* that night that kept her awake. A *feeling*, she said, that led her out to the driveway. A *feeling* that made her pick the lock on the door of Rocco's shiny new car and find me inside, bundled in a brown leather jacket, with the name Lucy scrawled on a piece of yellow paper pinned to the lapel.

I think I can safely say that if Rocco had known of my presence before my great-aunt did, he would have left me in the parking lot of Fumicelli's for some other unlucky gambler to stumble upon. Or maybe he would have simply thrown me into the Hudson River like a bad litter of pups. Instead, through divine providence or maybe just luck, I was delivered into the arms of four buxom Italian widows and one clairvoyant old maid, Rhodi. I was the child of their dreams. The child of their old age. Their one last chance to get it right.

Rhodi was my favorite aunt and the youngest of the five Sandoni daughters, all of whom were named after flowering Mediterranean shrubs: Mimosa, Hydrangea, Viburnum, Oleaster and Rhododendron, shortened fortunately to Mim, Hy, Vi, Olly and Rhodi. Unlike her other sisters, Rhodi was born with a harelip and a caul over her face, a thin veil of skin. A remnant from the other world. Like most caul babies, she grew into a gift of prophecy. She could hear voices and converse with spirits. She felt things in her bones, deep in her bones, and saw whole futures in the bottom of my great-aunts' china teacups.

"You'll have to excuse our sister Rhodi," Hy explained to visitors when Rhodi strode through the parlor with rosary beads wrapped around her neck or fresh fruit in her hair. "She marches to the beat of her own drum."

It was true. Rhodi did as she pleased. She loved Elvis and Led Zeppelin and read *National Geographic* magazines during Mass. She had a passion for bright pink lipstick and French perfume and always speaking the truth.

When I was old enough, Rhodi was the one who

told me I wasn't a Sandoni at all. She told me where I came from, that place of leather upholstery and chrome polish. My first home—the Buick.

"You must never forget your roots, dear, no matter what they are. Even if they rust and roll away. We all come from somewhere, even if we can never go back." Rocco sold my roots when I was six months old to pay off a gambling debt, but I used to imagine that my people—the ones who had *misplaced* me—were all Buicks. Strong, big-boned people with shiny teeth and deep, gravelly voices. My *people* were waiting out there in Buickland somewhere, I convinced myself. Somewhere west of Hamlin where the skies were bigger. They were waiting for *me*. And one day I would go looking for the Buicks and I would find them.

My childhood with the Sandonis was comfortable and, because of Rhodi, full of surprises. But it was very different from the one I would have had with the Buicks. My great-aunts loved me in their own peculiar way. With the exception of Mim, none had been blessed with children, so all their maternal instincts were poured forth upon me.

"Are you hungry, Lucy? Are you thirsty? Do you need an extra sweater?" They suffocated me with affection and fed me pasta six times a day. They dressed me like a little doll and sang me to sleep until I was almost ten.

On the other hand, my three uncles—Frank, Rocco and Onofrio—ignored me, which was probably the kindest thing they could have done. In fact, they took very little interest in me at all until my baby fat began to melt away and they suspected I might end up prettier than I'd started out.

"We have plans for you, little Lucretia. Big plans," I remember Rocco saying to me one morning at breakfast, through a mouthful of scrambled eggs. I was eight years old at the time and paying more attention to the egg hanging off his lip, wondering if it was going to fall off into his coffee, than to what he was really saying to me. Which was "We're planning the rest of your life for you, Lucretia . . . just wanted to let you know."

My uncles (Mim's sons) had no children of their own, and because all three of them had a sour disposition and were not in the least bit attractive, their prospects of catching a woman long enough to procure an offspring were slim. So, when I was nine years old, they declared me their official heir and began to groom me for the life they had in mind. They paid for braces to straighten my teeth and lessons in piano and etiquette. They sent me to St. Augustine's, a private school for girls, in the hopes that I would learn to be refined and graceful and well mannered, but it didn't work. I always said the first thing that came to my mind, and I hated wearing a uniform.

There was one thing I could do, though. One thing I loved more than anything else, and that was the violin. I was good at it. Maybe even better than good. Maybe great. But it didn't matter. My uncles didn't care if I could boil water. They didn't intend for me to excel in anything or take over their business one day as my great-aunts had hoped. The lessons and the fancy school were merely for show. They simply wanted to make me as attractive a package as possible to secure a prosperous match.

"Your face is your fortune, Lucretia," my uncles decided when they realized I would never be able to play the piano or host a social gathering. But it wasn't *my* fortune they were talking about. It was theirs.

By the time I turned seventeen, Hy, Vi, Mim and Olly had died and Rhodi was the only remaining barrier to my uncles' full-blown plans for me as the Sandoni heir. Rhodi was small and frail, but my uncles feared her more than they'd feared any of my other great-aunts. They thought she was a *fattucchiera*—a witch—and kept their distance. They wore the devil's horn around their necks, a little silver horn on a chain, to ward off her evil eye. But Rhodi didn't have an evil eye. She just had a plan.

Rhodi knew that one day a space would grow wide enough in the fabric of my small guarded life for me to squeeze through. She said strings of rosary beads on my behalf and taught me how to follow signs and read maps and train schedules. She knew that one day I would go looking for the Buicks and was forever preparing me for that precious moment when freedom finally presented itself.

In September, a few weeks before she died, Rhodi and I were sitting out on the front porch drinking lemonade when she had one of her spells. She closed her eyes and let her head fall onto the bosom of her floral housedress. In the past, Rhodi had been known to mumble to herself and even weep, but that day she sat still as a stone—as if trying to hear something from a long way off. She nodded a couple of times, asked for clarity from whatever spirit she was listening to, then opened her eyes and smiled at me.

"You'll be going away soon, Lucy," she said in her comforting way. "A sign will present itself to you. A path will be cleared."

And she was right.

Despite the way she looked and the way she mumbled and the way she swung her arms out to her sides when she walked, looking like some kind of strange arctic bird, I think Rhodi always knew exactly what she was doing.

CHAPTER TWO

IF RHODI HAD STILL BEEN ALIVE the afternoon of the fire, I would not have left. I would not have walked the backstreets of Hamlin that warm June evening after it had grown dark. I would not have bought a ticket at the Amstead train station to Albany, New York, and then to Chicago, and finally to California. I would not have left my three uncles standing in the parking lot of Sandoni Brothers Hosiery watching panty hose drift silently up to the tops of the streetlamps like wayward spirits.

If things had been different, I would have run home to the security of Rhodi's room on the third floor of the Sandoni brownstone on Connelly Street, put my head in her lap and asked for advice. But Rhodi wasn't there. That was part of her plan, too. She made sure she left before I did so I'd have no reason to stay. But I did have her words inside my head that night. "Trust yourself, Lucy," they said. "Trust the signs."

Rhodi and I believed in signs: the pattern of oak leaves on the sidewalk in early autumn, the remnants of a torn billboard, the name on a gum wrapper. "They're all messages from a strange and benevolent universe," Rhodi said, and we followed them whenever we could.

Once, when I was eight years old, Rhodi and I found a weather-beaten sign stapled to a telephone pole that simply read SALE AHEAD. We walked six and a half miles but never found it. Instead, we met a man with one arm who played the piccolo so sweetly it made us cry. Rhodi said signs could be like that sometimes, leading you places you never expected to go.

Before Rhodi died, I promised her two things: that I would wait for a sign and that I would finish school before I left the Sandonis. These were not easy promises to keep.

From the moment we came home from Rhodi's

funeral, things around the Sandoni brownstone began to change. I was suddenly guarded like a rare and valuable work of art. Rocco followed me to school and Frank picked me up from piano lessons. There was no time of the day or night that one of my uncles wasn't keeping an eye on me. Even my few friends began to notice.

"You're like one of the untouchables, Lucy," Lydia told me as she watched me punch in the twelve numbers on the keypad of Uncle Rocco's new security system to open the front door.

"Right," I said. "One of the untouchables." It was becoming increasingly difficult to escape from their constant surveillance.

"Where are you going, Lucretia?" my uncle Frank would ask me whenever he suspected I was trying to sneak out of the house for a walk. He could hear the creak of a door five miles away. I tried taking off my shoes and slipping out the back entrance. I even attempted climbing out my second-floor bedroom window and sliding down the roof.

"Are you meeting a boy?" his voice would boom out from the front porch, where he sat smoking one of his Cuban cigars.

"No, Uncle Frank," I'd yell, trying not to lose my grip on the edge of the rain gutter.

"What are you doing, then?"

"Nothing," I'd call out, crawling back over the windowsill into my room.

"Good," he'd answer. "Best idea I've heard all year." And that was the end of the conversation. I'd spend the evening in my room reading, and Uncle Frank would spend his no longer worried that I was going to meet a boy and ruin my chances at being the last virgin in Hamlin.

My uncles were men of few words and generally kept their thoughts and plans to themselves, especially concerning me. But one evening, I overheard them talking. There was an old-fashioned iron grate in the floor of my bedroom that opened into the ceiling of the parlor below. They'd forgotten to close it that night and I heard every word they said.

"I won't do it, Frank." Onofrio's voice sounded shaky.

"Listen, little brother. You'll do it because it's good for business. You'll do it or I'll cut you off."

"But she's just a kid, Frank. And that guy . . . he's bad news, you know he is. Besides, he's as old as . . . you are. In fact, he's *exactly* like you are." Of my three uncles, Onofrio was the only one who ever mustered any degree of human compassion.

"She's not a kid, Ono. She's eighteen," Rocco

chimed in. "It's time for her to earn her keep. Besides, we owe Mancini. Kill two birds with one stone."

"It's time," Frank said, agreeing with Rocco, "before she gets any ideas."

What ideas did they mean? I wondered. Did they think I hadn't had a hundred ideas in the last six months? If it hadn't been for my promise to Rhodi, I would have left long before. Even under their constant watch, there were holes I could have slipped through, if I'd wanted to. But I trusted Rhodi. I knew, from years of following signs with her, that timing was important.

The night before the fire, I had a dream. Rhodi was in it. She was standing on the roof of the brownstone, eating a salami wedge. Her hair was all done up with fruit and ribbons and papery bulbs of garlic. She waved to me, reached into the pocket of her housedress and drew forth a giant fireball. With all her strength, she lifted it above her head and hurled it into the sky over Hamlin. Then she sat down on the roof and started humming a little tune, an Italian lullaby she used to sing to me. Only the words were different. They were the lyrics of Rhodi's favorite Elvis song: "Burning Love."

I woke the next morning knowing that things had been set in motion. It was Saturday and I didn't go to work at the factory as I was supposed to. Instead, I walked downtown, bought an ice cream cone for lunch and went on a leisurely stroll along the ridge that overlooked Mill Street and Sandoni Brothers. I didn't want to go inside the factory that day. I just wanted to observe it from a distance.

My uncles' hosiery empire looked small from up on the ridge. The old brick facade appeared fragile, and the weathered letters that spelled out the name of the family's business were fading from rain and soot. It seemed charming in a way, not at all like the gloomy building it was on the inside, housing row upon row of industrial sewing machines and bare bulbs hanging in sockets from the ceiling.

The building was always empty on Saturdays, except for me. It was the one place my uncles didn't escort me to these days, because they knew I'd always show up. I was a creature of habit. I had been walking to Sandoni Brothers, rain or shine, for the past four years to dust Uncle Frank's office and do the payroll. If anyone was looking for me on Saturdays from noon until five p.m., they knew where to find me.

I was just imagining Frank's expression when he arrived at his office on Monday morning to discover that the books had not been done, and that there was no deposit slip in the safe, when I was thrown off my feet by an incredible blast. I landed on the ground next to my ice cream cone and a big pine tree. Four more explosions followed. When the fire whistle blew, I made myself get up, even though my knees felt like rubber. I crawled to the edge of the ridge and gazed down on the scene below. Black smoke was funneling up from the factory storage rooms. The smell of burning nylon filled the air.

As I stood watching Sandoni Brothers burn to the ground, I felt Rhodi's presence beside me. I remembered the story she used to tell me of Strega Nona, the Italian witch who opened her cupboard one morning expecting to see only a stale loaf of bread, but instead saw the whole world. That's what it was like. Like seeing my old life move aside and another step in to take its place.

I stood there looking down on that old life, on the dark clouds of smoke, the nylon panty hose blown up onto the branches of trees and my uncle Frank's Mercedes pulling into the parking lot. I watched Frank slowly open the door of the car and emerge into the smoky air. His eyes looked dazed, unbelieving, and I knew what he was thinking. I could tell even from where I stood on the ridge. I could tell by the way he narrowed his eyes and bit his lower lip. I could almost hear him thinking it. "All that money. All that time . . . for nothing."

Then I heard a voice say, "Go," quite loudly in my right ear. "Go now!" I turned, expecting to see my great-aunt's face, her long white hair blowing in the wind; a wise, benevolent figure. The kind of figure you'd expect to see at a moment like that. A moment when you were about to walk away from everything you'd ever known. But when I turned, there was no one beside me.

CHAPTER THREE

IT'S FUNNY THE WAY YOUR MIND plays tricks on you when you're tired; how you can see things that aren't there. Maybe it was the motion of the train, the sound of the wheels on the track, the rhythm. Maybe it was that lonely feeling that comes on at dusk and spreads slowly down the aisles. Whatever it was, in that state between waking and sleeping, I began to see them. In the early hours of the morning as the train raced through the small, bleak towns of upstate New York, and late at night when the lights from the rail yards flashed by, they came to visit me. Just when I'd stopped thinking about them for five minutes or ten minutes or a blissful twenty, they came. One after another the Sandoni women sat by my side.

The train had stopped. I pushed the little button on my watch that lit up the dial. "Three-forty-five a.m.," I groaned. It was raining lightly. The amber glow of the sodium lights along the track shone in through the window. I sat up and looked around the dimly lit car. There were only a few people sleeping in the far back rows. Everyone else had gotten off or found a sleeper for the night. I laid my head against the headrest.

What made those lights outside the window glow like that? I wondered, as my eyelids grew heavy. The lights seemed to be everywhere along the train line. They lit up the night in an eerie way. I was tired of them and tired of the train and tired of never sleeping for more than an hour without someone walking down the aisle or the train rattling around a curve. Sleep was my only relief from the images and thoughts that spun through my mind: the fire, the long trek through the woods, the fear that at any moment I would be recognized and sent back to Connelly Street. I wanted to enter a deep sleep. I reached up and drew the curtains, and turned on my side. That's when I saw it.

I strained my eyes in the dark.

Someone was sitting in the seat across from me, where a moment before there had been no one. Whoever it was, was small and round-shouldered. I stared, my heart beating like a frightened bird's.

The figure moved suddenly and eyes looked up at me. I let out a yell. It was Rhodi! I could tell even in the dark. Her hands, illuminated in a sliver of orange light, moved rhythmically along a string of rosary beads.

"Rhodi?" I whispered, hoping that just saying her name would wake me out of whatever dream I was in or cause her apparition to disappear.

"Hello, dear," she said, pulling the beads through her fingers and slipping them into the pocket of her housedress.

I sat up and rubbed my eyes. I swallowed and took a deep breath. I'd never been so glad and so afraid to see anyone in my whole life.

"I hope you don't mind, Lucy. But I had to come. While you're here." She glanced out the window. "In the middle of nowhere."

I looked out onto the deserted tracks and saw nothing but flat farmland spreading out forever into the darkness.

She held out a piece of butterscotch in the palm of

her hand. It was partially twisted and half melted, trying to escape from its wrapper.

"I'm sorry, dear," she whispered, trying to peel the torn paper off the sticky mound. "I've been carrying it for at least a month now and my pocket is as warm as an oven."

I gratefully accepted the soft disk from her sweaty palm and placed it on the center of my tongue the way I'd always done as a kid when Rhodi had offered me sweets. As the butter flavor spread through my mouth, a memory flooded in: I was sitting on the roof of the brownstone eating a bag of butterscotch the afternoon of Rhodi's funeral.

It had been one of those strange hot days in early October. The kind that made you think you were closer to summer than winter. The slate tiles on the roof burned the backs of my thighs, but I didn't care. I'd found a place to escape to for a while. Escape from the mourners who filed in and out of the front door bearing heavy platters of antipasti and plates of cannoli. Escape from my uncles brooding in the kitchen. Escape from the feeling of the house now that Rhodi was gone. A cold deserted feeling that not even Rhodi, with all her prayers and vigils to the Blessed Virgin, could have made warm again. For a brief time, sitting on that roof, I was above it all. I was a little closer to Rhodi and a little farther away from the life that awaited me in the empty rooms below. A life ruled by the uncles and their *associates*. A life of secrets and strangers in the parlor and the incessant talk of money.

Butterscotch had always been Rhodi's favorite. Maybe that's why I brought a whole bag of it up there that day. So I'd never forget her.

"Well, Rhodi," I said, crunching the candy between my teeth. "We did it."

"You did it, Lucy."

"With a little help from you."

Rhodi smiled and looked away. "I don't know what you're talking about, dear."

"The sign. You know. The big, smoky sign back in Hamlin was the right sign . . . wasn't it?"

"What do you think?"

"Well, it certainly changed things."

"Are you worrying about the boys, Lucy?" Rhodi asked, referring to my uncles. "Because if you are, you shouldn't be."

It wasn't my uncles I was thinking about. It was everyone else: my teachers at St. Augustine's, Lydia, the firemen . . . myself. It struck me as I snuck out of town under cover of night that the all-consuming nature of this sign had left me in the rather uncomfortable position of being . . . dead . . . to everyone who knew me.

"You were ready, Lucy, weren't you?"

I'd been ready forever. In fact, I'd never let myself get very close to anyone in Hamlin. Even Lydia, whom I'd known most of my life, I'd kept at arm's length. What was the point of getting involved, if I was just going to leave one day anyway?

"But, still, Rhodi. It was awfully final."

"I've come to believe, Lucy, that the only reliable way out of the Sandoni family is to die. It seems strange at first, dear. But you'll get used to it. Besides, you cannot waste a moment worrying about what's behind you. You must look ahead now. You have to find the Buicks, remember? Trust me. Everyone will be fine."

"What about me, Rhodi? Will I be fine, too?"

She didn't answer. She bent over and started picking at something under her seat. When she'd been alive, Rhodi had had the unusual habit of always fidgeting with things—strings and beads and knots—collecting little treasures to fill her pockets. Finally, she surfaced with a large wad of chewing gum and a rusty paper clip. Looking up at me, she said, "What, dear?"

"Will I be all right?"

"You mustn't be afraid now, Lucy. No matter what any of my sisters say, you keep going." She broke into song then.

"Pound for pound oh yeah and
Ounce for ounce love is all that really counts . . ."

As she sat there singing her heart out, I began to wonder where she'd come from and how she'd gotten there.

If this was a dream, it was one I would never forget. If it was real, I was worried for my sanity. Perhaps this is what happens when you ride on a train all night without really sleeping. Maybe I was hallucinating from ingesting too many Milky Way bars, which was all I'd eaten since the morning before.

"Are you real, Rhodi?" I asked after she'd finished the verse. I reached out my hand and touched the hem of her housedress. It felt like cotton.

"Yes, I am," she said, dropping the piece of chewed bubble gum into her pocket. "I'm as real as any."

"As any what?"

"As any on my side. Among spirits."

"Is that what you are, Rhodi? A spirit?"

Rhodi laughed. "Well, isn't that what we all are, my dear? Aren't we all just spirits trying to find our way?"

I stared into her gray eyes. Actually, she was almost all gray, in a way. There was a little hint of color coming off the rose blossom in the pattern of her dress, but the rest faded into gray and Rhodi herself seemed a little thin around the edges; a little blurry.

"I'm fading, dear. I'll be going soon. It requires a bit of work to take shape again. I really don't look anything like this anymore."

"You don't? What do you look like, then?" I asked.

Rhodi laughed again and, as her bosom jiggled, the blurriness spread up to her knees and down her arms.

"It's a little hard to explain, Lucy. I'll get into it at another time."

"Will there *be* another time? Will you come back, Rhodi?" I could hear the desperation in my voice. I tried to touch her sleeve, but it felt like only a cool breeze.

"Keep your eyes open, Lucy. There are more signs."

"But I can't find the signs without *you*, Rhodi. Not unless they knock me off my feet."

Rhodi smiled. She pulled a Cracker Jack box out of her pocket and ripped open the top. Dipping her fading fingers inside, she pulled up a handful of caramel corn.

And then the form of Rhodi wasn't there anymore. I got down and searched under the seats, feeling for some sign of her: the cool breeze, the rosary beads. Nothing.

The train jerked forward and the car lights flicked on and off and the motion began. That strange train motion that never seemed to stop for long. Taking me farther away or farther toward something. I wasn't sure which. I wasn't sure of anything. I pulled my knees up to my chin and gathered my sweater around my shoulders. Rain hit hard against the window. I could still feel Rhodi around me. I thought I could even smell her—an odd combination of lavender perfume and garlic. I closed my eyes and let the rhythm of the train lull me into a fitful sleep.

CHAPTER FOUR

RHODI WAS LIKE THE GHOST of Jacob Marley warning Ebenezer Scrooge of more spirits to come. In fact, if I thought getting off the train would have stopped any of them from coming, I'd have jumped off right away. But once again Rhodi's words came back to me, clearer than before. I wasn't dead. And in a way, neither were they. My four remaining great-aunts reminded me of this fact. They came later that night. As their words filled my head, I tried to remember what Rhodi had told me.

My great-aunts, with the exception of Rhodi, had lived their lives under a complex mixture of fear, duty, guilt and belief that Italian food could cure almost any human ill. Mim, Hy, Vi and Olly: the four well-endowed Sicilian sisters in black dresses, with lace mantillas covering their heads, squeezed into the three seats surrounding me, pushing at each other for more room.

"Now, Lucretia, dear," they began in unison. Then one after another they chimed in their advice, echoing each other's opinions, nodding and occasionally patting me on the arm to reassure me that not all was lost. I could easily make amends and save my old life.

"You were always such a good little girl, Lucretia," they went on. "Always did what you were told. Never complained." It was just before dawn and the train was somewhere in the middle of Illinois. Grain silos stood far off in the distance like lonely gray giants.

Olly patted my arm. "Don't worry, little doll, you'll find a way to make it right," she said. "You'll go back home and everything will be fine. The neighbors will understand." I laughed to myself. Just like Olly to be worried about what the neighbors would think.

"Things changed after you died," I tried explaining to them. They stared at me as if I were speaking another language. "You know, it wasn't so great on Connelly Street by the time I left. I'm eighteen now!

You've all been gone for a while." Olly poked Vi to scoot over and give her more room. Hy snorted and folded her arms across her chest. They weren't listening to me. They never did.

"I remember saying to Harry Cerulli one day," Mim said as if I hadn't spoken at all. "Do you remember Harry, Lucy?" I nodded. Harry Cerulli was the mayor of Hamlin, and Mim thought he was the smartest man on the face of the earth. "I said, 'Harry, Lucretia is going to do well in life. She'll take over the factory. She'll make out better than all of us. You just wait and see.' "

My great-aunts didn't know about the Buicks. They thought I was content to be a Sandoni for the rest of my life. They never gave much thought to the power my uncles might try to wield over me after they were gone. They just assumed I wanted to stay in Hamlin and take over the business. Rhodi was the only one who knew the truth.

"Oh, Lucretia." Mim's voice broke. She pulled a hankie from the bosom of her black wool dress. The same one she'd worn since my uncle Vittorio died forty years before. The rest of them followed suit and pulled out their own monogrammed handkerchiefs.

"Oh, Lucretia. What will become of you now?" they all wailed.

"I'll be fine. Really . . . I will," I said, trying to

convince them and myself even as I said it. "I was suffocating back there. You must remember how it was? Rocco. Frank. Onofrio. They wanted to marry me off to one of their horrible business associates. I would have died if I'd stayed."

"But you would have been safe, Lucretia," Hy whispered. "You would have had a warm house and plenty of food and security. You would've had a bank account. We all worked hard to give you those things and now look." She gestured with open palms toward my rumpled shirt and tousled hair. "You've thrown it all away!" They started wailing loudly again and blowing their noses. I looked around the train car, but no one seemed to hear anything; they were all sleeping.

My great-aunts were right about one thing, though. Life at the Sandonis' was at least predictable.

When I was little, Hy would lay out all my clothes for me on the bed in the morning right down to my underwear and say, "Lucretia, it's Tuesday. Plaid dress, white socks, blue underwear Tuesday." Until two days ago, I'd always known exactly what would happen in my life on Tuesday and Wednesday and every other day of the week. From the time I woke up until the time I went to bed, I knew what I'd be doing. Now I didn't even know where I was going.

I wondered what would happen if I just stayed on this train for the rest of my life. If I never got off, I'd never have to decide where to go. I'd never have to decide anything. The train would decide for me.

"Do you at least know where you're going?" asked Vi. "Do you have some kind of plan?" She wiped her eyes, slipped on her bifocals and looked down her nose at me. She was a stout woman with broad shoulders and wide hips. She was the one who'd made sure the pantry was always full and that everyone got to work at the factory on time.

"Well, I'm not certain yet." They stared at me . . . waiting. "I've been looking for signs." I knew this was a mistake the moment I said it.

Olly let out a deep sigh. "Oh, Lucretia. Not that nonsense. Are you going to go around following signs your whole life like our crazy sister? Look where that got her. Nowhere. No family. No children. A life wasted."

I felt as if I might be sick. I wanted to tell them all to leave, but I didn't know how. One by one, they put their hands on my forehead.

"You're overtired and overwrought, Lucretia," they chimed in together. "You need a good night's sleep in a decent bed and a square meal. Then maybe you'll come to your senses."

I wanted to say that I *had* come to my senses, but the four sisters suddenly began to fade before I could utter a word.

That's the way it always happened. I could never speak my mind with my great-aunts. They had a way of rendering me speechless and then leaving the room before I could respond. Maybe it was the sheer force of their collective presence.

"We'll be back, Lucretia," they said as they stood up and moved abruptly down the aisle toward the dining car. "Don't do anything foolish. Remember, you have your reputation to . . ." Their voices trailed off and they were gone as quickly as they'd come.

"*Union Station*," the conductor's voice blared over the intercom, jolting me from my few precious moments of sleep. "Next stop, *Union Station*. Passengers making connections in Chicago, please move to the forward three cars. Thank you for riding the Lake Shore Limited and have a safe journey."

A wave of dread passed through me as I sat up in my seat. I stared out the window at the rain and the inevitable signs of a big city approaching. The flat landscape had given way to factories and oil refineries and bridges with graffiti scrawled on every bare surface.

The train was stopping and I had to make a decision. I had two thousand dollars in my backpack—money Rhodi left for me, stashed in her room under the statue of the Virgin of Guadalupe. I had intended to deposit it in the bank the morning of the fire, but never got around to it. Which was lucky. With Rhodi's gift, I could now go anywhere. So why was I so afraid?

I felt a growing panic as the people around me collected their luggage and folded up their newspapers. I crossed my fingers and closed my eyes to say a prayer. It was the only one I could think of: *Dear St. Anthony, Please come around, something's lost and must be found.* I knew this was a totally inappropriate prayer for such an occasion. Rhodi only prayed to St. Anthony when she needed help finding small objects like rings or my uncle Rocco's car keys. Still, I thought St. Anthony might expand his repertoire to include a person who had lost their way or lost their life or possibly even lost their mind. All three categories probably applied to me at the moment. Maybe St. Anthony would give me a sign. I needed one desperately.

In the pouch on the back of the seat in front of me was a brochure for the California Zephyr, a train that traveled to San Francisco. The photographs highlighted the beautiful canyons, prairies and mountains along the line. They seemed like the kind of places where the Buicks might live. And the idea of a zephyr, a gentle breeze, appealed to me. I might have been plunked down at birth in the backseat of an automobile, but perhaps my luck was changing and this train would gracefully blow me into my real life.

When the train stopped, I went directly into Union Station and bought a ticket to California. At the very least, it would give me more time to figure out my next step. I caught the Zephyr at 1:18 p.m. and settled myself into a new seat by a new window and watched the rain-soaked landscape of western Illinois pass by. As I sat there, a feeling came over me. The same kind of feeling I'd had when Rhodi and I had been on the trail of some new adventure on the streets of Hamlin.

It was the feeling that some bigger force was working its way through me, beckoning me forward. I had no idea where it was taking me and I didn't care. For a little while, at least, all my thoughts were suspended. All the voices of the past were silent, and I knew one thing for sure. I couldn't go back now, even if I wanted to.

CHAPTER FIVE

THE CALIFORNIA ZEPHYR STOPPED in Ottumwa, Iowa, where a handful of new passengers got on. I watched them take their seats. I wondered where they were headed. What their stories were. Maybe because I was running away, I looked for that in others. Potential runaways. I found myself inventing all kinds of lives for these people, especially the ones who sat down next to me. I hoped my faraway look would discourage them from asking too many questions. The last two days were catching up with me, and my midnight conversations with deceased family members were taking their toll.

"Is this yours? I found it on the floor." A young guy stood beside me, holding my backpack in his hand.

"Yes," I said, reaching for it. "Thank you." It was the one article besides the clothes on my back that remained of my old life. I grabbed it by the strap, forgetting that the zipper was undone, and all my earthly possessions spilled out onto the floor. All the things I had so carelessly thrown inside the day before the fire lay in the aisle for everyone to see.

Together we gathered up my wallet, keys to the factory, a pack of gum, six pencils, two pens, a tube of Chapstick, a hair clip and the remnants of a candy bar wrapper.

"Where are you going?" he asked when we'd finally both settled into our seats.

I took a deep breath. "California, I think."

It was the logical destination. The final destination. He cocked his head. He was the youngest of my seatmates so far. Maybe twenty or twenty-two. He had the kind of rugged face that looked as if he spent a lot of time outdoors. A little sunburned and ruddy. Blue eyes. Wild, curly blond hair.

"You think?" he asked.

"Well, you never know what might happen," I said.

"Like what?"

I suddenly thought of Aunt Mim, who was afraid of everything. I went over her disaster list in my head. The one she repeated to me every time I was about to do something she considered slightly dangerous: What if there was an earthquake? What if I lost my wallet? What if the world ended tomorrow? What if? What if? What if?

"Oh, I don't know. Derailment . . . train robbery . . . tornado . . . anything, really."

He laughed and opened a bag of garlic potato chips. "Would you like one?" he asked. I hesitated. "If you're going to get robbed or derailed, what's there to lose?" he went on. "You won't even have time to get fat."

"Good point," I said, reaching into the bag and stuffing a chip into my mouth. Potato chips were so delicious. Vi never let me eat them. "Terrible for your complexion, Lucretia," she would say, handing me a dish of carrot sticks instead. She would have had a fit if she could have seen all the junk food I'd been gorging on since Hamlin.

"Where are *you* going?" I asked, dipping my hand back into the bag for a fistful of chips.

"Kansas," he said. I nodded as if I knew where Kansas was in relation to anything, but I didn't. I actually had very little idea what was west of Hamlin (besides Buickland, of course). I have a mental block when it comes to geography. Sister Graviola, who taught history at St. Augustine's, used to tell Aunt Hy that I had no memory for historical facts and wouldn't know the Mediterranean from the Red Sea if I drove into them. This is not entirely true. It's just that I have little interest in studying things that don't apply to my immediate circumstances. If I were planning a trip to the south of France, I would be interested in knowing more about the Mediterranean, but for now, why clutter my mind with useless facts?

"So, what's Kansas like?" I asked. "Is it similar to Iowa?" I had grown rather fond of Iowa. The gentle green hills we'd passed through that afternoon looked comforting. Predictable. I was hoping the landscape would remain exactly the same until I reached the mountains.

"Kansas is like an ocean," he said. "A big, dry, windswept ocean. It's so flat you could never get lost there. Everything is right out in the open. Oil wells and dust for miles and miles. And great weather!" He seemed excited about all that openness, but I found the whole idea unsettling. Vulnerable.

Big, open places were not where I wanted to be at the moment. I couldn't shake the feeling that I was on the run and that my uncles were out there somewhere looking for me. Could I possibly have escaped so easily?

"So what do you do in Kansas?" I pressed. I liked hearing him talk. It kept my mind from worry. None of my uncles talked much. They grunted and stared and occasionally gestured with their hands for more food. But they never talked about anything meaningful.

"I do meteorological work. I was visiting a friend in Ottumwa and my truck broke down. I have to pick up a piece of equipment in Kansas and check out some weather while I'm there, so the train seemed like the best alternative. Here," he said, reaching into his pocket and pulling out a small white business card. "Do you have a pen?"

"Sure." I fumbled around inside my backpack and handed him one.

"I have a new number," he said, writing it on the back of the card. When he finished, he read the side of the pen. " 'Sandoni Brothers, Hamlin, New York,' " he said. "What do they make?"

At the mention of the Sandonis, I felt all the blood in my body drain into my feet and I knew that if I hadn't been sitting down, I would have passed out.

"It's—it's just a pen I picked up somewhere," I said, staring at him. He nodded and I could tell, with relief, that the Sandoni name meant nothing to him.

Why would it? Outside New York State, I doubted anyone had heard of my family's business.

He twirled the pen in his hands. "I have a lot of pens like this. I never know where they come from," he admitted. I felt too shaken to speak. How careless of me. I should have thrown that pen into the woods back in Amstead. I'd be more cautious from now on.

He flipped the little white card over and handed it to me. "My dad made these up for me." *Brian McNeil, Meteorologist, Cracker Jack, Inc., Gardenia, Iowa.*

"Thanks," I said, finding my voice and taking his card. "Cracker Jack," I whispered, remembering Rhodi's midnight snack.

"That's my dog's name. Cracker Jack. He's a retriever. I named the business after him. Seemed like a good idea at the time."

I nodded. "No offense or anything," I said, "but you don't seem old enough to be a meteorologist."

He laughed. "No offense taken. For the kind of work I do, it's better to be young and fearless. Or as my father would say, 'young and foolish.' "

"Your father doesn't approve of your occupation?"

"He's happy I have a degree and a profession. He just doesn't understand why I can't be content sitting behind a desk watching weather patterns on a computer screen."

"And you're not?"

"No, ma'am."

"What exactly do you do, then?"

He lowered his voice and looked behind us as if he were about to divulge a deep secret. "I chase storms," he whispered.

"You chase them?" He nodded. "Where do you chase them?"

"Anywhere they want to go."

"Don't they have some predictable course?"

"Nope. Each storm is unique—like a snowflake. It has a distinct pattern and life of its own. How it starts, how long it will last, nobody really knows. You can make predictions and send out warnings, but in the end, nature will do as it pleases. That's why I can't sit behind a screen and watch all that amazing weather happen. I have to be in the middle of it. Especially the wind. Funnels are my specialty."

"Funnels?" I asked.

"Funnels," he repeated. "Twisters. Tornadoes."

"Isn't that kind of dangerous? I mean tornadoes are so out of control!"

"I know." A big smile spread across his face. "That's what I love about them." I raised my eyebrows. "Did you know that some tornadoes have been known to rip off the front of a person's shirt," he went on, "but not the back? Or suck off one shoe and not the other?"

"You're kidding."

He shook his head. "There are even some funnels called waterspouts that can pick up fish from a river, carry them miles overland and drop them on a town."

"I find that hard to believe."

"Cross my heart and hope to die, it's true."

I laughed. "Are you saying it can rain fish?"

"You bet." I looked at him cross-eyed. "You think I'm crazy, don't you? That's okay. Most people think that, when I tell them what I do for a living. Maybe that's a good sign."

I sat up at the mention of signs. "Why?"

"My grandma used to say that when people thought she was crazy for doing what she loved, that's when she knew she was doing the right thing."

"What did she do?"

"She made kites."

The image of an old woman making kites and her grandson chasing storms seemed to fit perfectly.

"Well, for what it's worth, I don't think you're crazy. Compared to my life at the moment, yours seems pretty normal. I have to say, though, that chasing storms is probably the last thing you'd ever catch me doing."

"Why is that?"

"Ever since I saw *The Wizard of Oz* as a kid, I've been terrified of tornadoes."

"There are more earthquakes than tornadoes in California."

"What about Iowa?"

"About thirty tornadoes a year in Iowa. More in Texas, Kansas and Oklahoma. I end up spending most of my time driving to places other than Iowa. But I grew up in Gardenia and all my family is there. I'm a hometown boy who's never home."

Somehow I could picture his family: a big, friendly, happy-go-lucky clan that got together for barbecues and Sunday dinners. Next to Brian, I felt like a leaf blowing in the wind, a plant that had pulled itself from its pot, roots and all.

"Sometimes the people who are most afraid of storms are the ones who end up chasing them," he said.

I was going to ask him what he meant by that, but he suddenly turned in his seat and grabbed his jacket.

"Hey, all this talk of storms is making me hungry. I'm going to get some real food. Want to join me?"

I shook my head. For some reason my stomach was all jumpy.

"Well, then," he said, standing up and putting his jacket under his arm. "I'm getting a sleeper at the next stop, so in case I don't see you again, it was nice meeting you, Miss . . ." He waited for my name.

"Lucy," I said.

"Just Lucy?" he asked.

"Lucy . . . Buick." I couldn't believe I'd said it.

He repeated my name slowly as if he were trying to see how it sounded.

"Well, Lucy Buick," he said. "I hope we meet again. If you end up anywhere in Iowa and you see a big storm coming, don't hesitate to give me a ring and I'll chase it down for you, okay?"

"Okay." I laughed.

He extended his hand toward me. I looked at it before giving him mine. I was almost sure I'd feel something if I shook it, the way Rhodi used to whenever she met someone important. She'd feel a kind of vibration in her palm that sent a little shock up her arm. I took his hand, but there was no vibration or shock of any kind, just a little extra heat.

Gardenia was the next stop. I reached my hand into my pocket and found a nickel. I took it out and studied it. Heads to stop. Tails to go on. I closed my eyes and flipped the coin onto the now-vacant seat next to me. It bounced once and landed, revealing the strong profile of Thomas Jefferson and the words *In God We Trust* in an arc before his face. I looked out the window as tiny pieces of milkweed wishes blew up onto the glass, a few sticking in the moisture around the frame from the previous night's rain. It almost looked as if it were snowing out, and for a moment I imagined that it was. What would Iowa be like, I wondered, in the snow?

GARDENIA, the sign over the train platform read. Maybe there was some meaning in the name of this town. It was certainly more interesting than Cleveland or Galesburg. I remembered seeing a gardenia once in a shop in Hamlin. Aunt Mim pointed it out to me. A flower with a pretty white blossom.

I'd been wondering what platform I would eventually stop at. I thought of all the towns that had gone by and all the people who had gotten off at their logical destinations. Ever since Amstead, I'd secretly envied every one of those people.

I glanced at Brian McNeil's card in my hand. *Well, Rhodi,* I thought, *I hope I'm doing the right thing here.* Even as I thought this, I knew what Rhodi's answer would be: "There's no such thing as the right thing. There's just the only thing. That's what you're doing, Lucy. The only thing."

I patted my backpack and, along with two teenagers and an elderly gentleman, stepped out onto the cement platform. Together, we stood watching the train doors close and the wheels slowly begin to turn again. We kept our eyes on the train as it disappeared down the tracks, moving on without us. Then we turned and sort of smiled at each other as if we all understood what we'd just done. The train was no longer taking care of us. We were on our own.

CHAPTER SIX

IT WASN'T HARD TO FIND signs in Gardenia. They were everywhere at the train depot. Stapled to bulletin boards and pasted around poles. Signs for new tractors and feed storage and pigs for sale. I'd never seen so many signs in one place before. *This must be some kind of test*, I thought. I needed Rhodi for this part, but she was nowhere to be found.

"Are you lost?" a voice asked.

Two men with briefcases walked up beside me. I

had no idea where they came from. One was reed thin, with bad skin. The other was short, with thick black hair. The thin man had eyes that wandered off in two different directions, so I wasn't sure at first if he was speaking to me.

"No, I don't think I'm lost. At least not yet," I answered. "I'm just looking for something." I continued to scan the walls, hoping they would go away. They didn't. They lingered around the platform in deep conversation until the short man worked up the nerve to approach me.

"What do you think is going to happen at the end of the world?" he asked.

I stared at him. I had no idea what was going to happen in the next five minutes, let alone at the end of the world. But there was something so sincere about the way he'd asked the question, I thought I should at least give it my best shot for his sake. He really seemed to want to know. I tried to think about what Mim always told me. The end of the world was one of her favorite topics.

"Well, let's see . . ." I cleared my throat and switched the backpack onto my other shoulder. "After the beasts and the plagues and the fire and the gnashing of teeth and all that, I guess . . ." Both of the men looked excited by what I was saying, but then my mind drew a blank. Suddenly, Rhodi's opinion came out of my mouth instead of Mim's. "I guess God is going to sit us all down and say, 'Okay, let's try this whole thing over again. Only this time, don't screw up, and let the women be in charge.' " I laughed. They didn't. The short man drew a colorful pamphlet out of his pocket and handed it to me.

"I think you should read this," he said solemnly. I could tell by the expression on his face that I had not given him the answer he had hoped for.

"Thanks," I said, taking the pamphlet. "Good luck finding the answer to your question." They looked confused. "About the end of the world, I mean."

The short man nodded. "Oh, yes, right."

"Maybe someday soon we can talk about the Lord Jehovah in greater detail," the thin man said as I began to walk away. I knew they didn't want to let me go. I'm sure it wasn't every day in Gardenia, Iowa, that they came across a genuine lost soul like me.

"That would be nice," I said, and ducked around the corner. Fortunately they didn't follow.

Out of sheer exhaustion, I picked the strangest and most hopeless sign I could find. I had to start somewhere. I settled on a hand-painted board hanging from the window of an abandoned gas station ten yards from the train platform, which read:

Ma Sparling's Motor Lodge
Chicken Dinners ~ Night Crawlers
Hourly Rates

The sign looked as if it had survived at least one tornado and quite a few hard winters. At the bottom, in small print, it said: *1.4 miles past* . . . The rest had been washed away.

One point four miles seemed very far at the moment. My body felt as if it weighed five hundred pounds and my clothes, which I'd been wearing for the past two days, were starting to adhere to my skin.

It was early evening, but the day had been hot and the cicadas in the cornfield behind me were still hard at work, buzzing their little hearts out. Two choices lay before me: I could stay out here with the cicadas in the fading light, or I could see if Ma Sparling was still alive and had a shower I could use. A rusty pickup streaked by, covering me in a cloud of red dust, and I made my decision. I picked up my backpack and started walking.

Ma Sparling's was nowhere to be found 1.4 miles in any direction, but there was a motor lodge named Lila's perched off the main road that advertised homemade pies and welcomed truckers. I ventured up the driveway. Aunt Vi would have been horrified by the very sight of the place. But it looked great to me. Besides, when you're dead, you don't really have to worry about what's respectable anymore.

The farther away from Hamlin I traveled, the more I realized how strange my life had been on Connelly Street, listening to the advice of great-aunts and uncles whose major preoccupation in life was maintaining the quality of their nylon to keep women's legs bound and protected. That world seemed very small to me now.

I looked through the broken screen door of the front office. No one was around. There was, however, a loud humming coming from somewhere behind the building. I followed it and peered around the doorframe of a small laundry room. A woman was bent over an ancient washing machine, her hands placed on its sides as if giving it a massage. I couldn't see her face, but from the posture of her body, I could tell she was in deep concentration.

"MMMMmmmmmmm," she hummed along with the whir of the machine. "AHHHHhhhhh. OOOOOOOOOhhhhhh. LAAAAAhhhhhh." The pitch of her voice rose higher and higher. I stepped back from the door. "Yes! Yes!" she screamed. I jumped. "One more, Ramona." Her arms sprang into the air. "Yes! Yes! Yes! Hallelujah!" She banged the top of the washing machine with her fist. "Thank you, thank you. Amen!" The woman lowered her face to the lid and gently kissed it.

Maybe I didn't need that shower so badly after all. I tried to move away quietly, but at the sound of my feet, the woman turned and looked at me. She didn't seem surprised by my presence, just curious. I raised my hand to my chest and gave a little wave.

"Hi," I said, feeling as if I'd just been caught eavesdropping on some kind of personal religious ritual. "I didn't mean to disturb you."

"Not disturbing me," the woman said, turning back to the machine and pulling a small wrench out of her pocket.

"Are you Lila?" I asked, looking at the tattoo on her left forearm—a big *L* inside a heart.

"Yes, ma'am. Lila Fortune. I'd shake your hand if I had a free one," she said into the barrel of the machine. "Need a room?"

"Yes, please, just for a day or two?"

"Passing through?" She fiddled with something on the top of the old machine. "I need a crescent wrench for this," she mumbled. "Maybe a hairpin will do." She pulled a caramel-colored bobby pin from the swirl of frizzled blond hair and stretched it open with her teeth. "You'll probably want clean sheets?"

"That would be nice," I said. "If it isn't too much trouble."

"Well, if Ramona makes it through this cycle, you're set and so am I."

She popped a long black rubber tube from the back panel of the machine and handed it to me. "Burned out. She needs a new belt. Heard it on the rinse cycle," she said, fitting a new one on. "I call this old gal Ramona 'cause I've always liked the name. Spitfire kind of name, don't you think?"

I nodded.

"Ramona and I have been through almost everything together," Lila went on. "Five husbands, two fires and a gallbladder operation, but she still keeps going. And so do I."

Somehow I could believe this. Lila looked as if she had seen a lot in her life. She reminded me of Olly's friend Frieda Schultz, who'd had *six* husbands. Frieda and Lila had the same kind of bleached-blond hair and full figure and no doubt smoked three packs of cigarettes a day. I could tell Lila was a heavy smoker. Her voice was deep and raspy and all the lines in her skin ran together at her mouth, like tributaries to a river. But there was something warm about her, too. Something kind.

"Ramona was my inheritance from the little old lady who owned the place before I did."

"Ma Sparling?"

"How do you know Ma?"

"I saw the sign down at an old gas station."

"Well, I'll be. Is that sign still swinging?" I nodded. "Ma was a great old gal. Passed on a number of years ago. This place was pretty run-down when I got it, but Ramona's always hung in there. Every once in a while, she gets a kink in her system, though, and I have to straighten her out." Lila loaded a bundle of sheets into the machine, pulled the dial and closed the lid. It began to fill with water.

"It always works best to make the diagnosis without taking her all apart," Lila continued. "Just a little patience. That's all that's required. This morning it was a bad belt. Last month a bad hose. I can do it with tractors, fourteen-wheelers, most whatever drives in here," she explained. "It's a lot less complicated than people. All I can do for people is give them a warm meal and a clean room and send 'em on their way. Can't fix their insides, though sometimes I wish I could."

"I just need a room, that's all," I said, hoping she wasn't thinking I had come for anything more complicated than that.

"Hungry?"

"Starving."

"I like a woman who doesn't mince words." She took the belt out of my hand and waved me to follow her.

✣ ✣ ✣

Lila led me into a bright little kitchen filled to the brim with everything you could imagine. Vi would have fainted at the sight of it, but I found it strangely comforting. There were stacks of dirty dishes and dirty laundry, newspapers everywhere, car parts in the sink and a whole table dedicated to drying bunches of long spindly flowers. But whatever was cooking smelled wonderful.

"I'm trying out a new recipe and you're my first victim. Sit down, honey, wherever you can."

I moved a pile of newspapers and a bowl of old chili off a chair and placed them on the floor. A small hairy creature the size of a teacup wandered over and sniffed at the crusted bowl.

"Rufus! Get your face out of there. Do you want to kill yourself?" Lila swooped down on the little thing, picked it up and tucked it under her arm. She held its face in her hand, forcing it to look into her eyes. *"Rufus, no chili for you!"* She pronounced each word loudly and slowly as if she were speaking to someone who didn't hear well or understand English. I wasn't sure which category Rufus fell under. He looked up at Lila apologetically through his long shaggy bangs.

"Almost lost him last winter when he got hold of an avocado," Lila went on as she picked up the bowl and placed it in the sink. She put Rufus down and pulled a cigarette from her shirt pocket, lit it, took a long drag and blew the smoke into the air above my head. "Lord, I've never seen a dog throw up anything quite that color before." She watched the smoke circle around until it disappeared, took another drag and stubbed the cigarette out in the bottom of the old bowl of chili. "So, what will it be? Some of my new red pepper hash or a chicken salad sandwich?"

I tried to put the little dog's digestive habits out of my mind. "I guess, hmm . . . I'll try the hash?"

"Hash it is!" Lila grabbed a clean bowl. Rufus whimpered and crawled under my chair.

I'd never had hash before. Growing up in an Italian family, I mostly ate pasta. It came in a hundred different shapes and sizes: capellini, fettuccini, linguini, rigatoni and so on forever. Fortunately, I hadn't seen any pasta since I'd left Hamlin. I wasn't sure if I could ever eat any again without thinking of the Sandonis, which I was trying hard not to do. But sitting in a good-smelling kitchen brought me right back to Connelly Street. To Olly's marinara sauce and Hy's homemade panini.

"Here you go, honey," Lila said, lowering a full bowl before me. I picked up my fork.

"Don't you want ketchup?" Lila plunked down a bottle.

"Sure."

"And mustard. You can't eat hash without a little mustard."

"Right, mustard." The plate was steaming and smelled good, but after I'd doused it with ketchup *and* mustard, the sight was less than appetizing.

"Go on, honey. It won't bite you." I gave Lila a weak smile and dug my fork in. Lila watched. Rufus emerged from beneath my chair and looked up at me, expectant. I put the fork in my mouth, aware of the two pairs of eyes staring at me, and I smiled to myself. This afternoon I'd been on a train headed for California, and now I was sitting in a kitchen in the middle of Iowa eating my very first bowl of red pepper hash with a woman who talked to washing machines and a hairy little creature who had a fetish for avocados. I'm sure Rhodi was hovering around me, chuckling. This could only be her doing.

"It's good," I said, looking up at Lila. "It's very good." I wasn't saying this just to be nice. It was actually delicious and hot, a welcome change from train food.

"Never knew anyone who could turn down a bowl of my hash. Soul food," Lila said with satisfaction. "Though I wouldn't let Rufus get anywhere near it." She picked Rufus up and sat down across from me. "This breed has a delicate constitution," she explained.

"What kind is it?" I wasn't sure if I should ask

'What kind of *dog* is it?' because I wasn't sure Rufus qualified as a dog. He looked more like a giant guinea pig.

"This is a Lhasa apso. They're from China."

"Oh," I said through a mouthful of hash.

"What's your name, honey?"

"Lucy," I said.

"Don't you have a last name?"

I nodded and swallowed. "Buick." There, I'd said it again. Each time it sounded a little more natural and a little less like a lie. I couldn't help feeling that when I uttered their name, the Buicks, wherever they were, were drawn a little closer to me.

"Like the car?"

"Just like the car."

"Well, Lucy Buick," Lila said, running her hand over Rufus's head. "We're mighty glad you found us."

CHAPTER SEVEN

LILA'S MOTOR LODGE SAT CLOSE to the main road, and all through the night trucks pulled into the parking lot, their lights shining in through my window. I was exhausted but I couldn't sleep. I felt as if I hadn't quite landed in this small town. I was sure my soul was still somewhere between here and Hamlin looking for me. I imagined it wandering around in the darkness, in the cornfields, calling my name.

During daylight, Lila's had felt welcoming and safe, but at night, I could hear strange noises coming from the other rooms: men coughing and a bottle smashing. I pushed a desk against the door and bolted it twice. I picked up the New Gideon Bible from the nightstand for comfort, but I kept turning to passages about pestilence, so I closed it and looked around the room for a hairbrush. I hadn't brought anything in my backpack that resembled a toothbrush or a bar of soap, and Lila's wasn't the kind of establishment to supply travelers with incidentals. If you didn't bring it, you didn't have it.

I sat on the edge of the bed in my underwear, trying to dry my shirt with an old blow-dryer someone had left behind. Every few minutes the dryer began to overheat and smoke and I had to stop and let it rest, but I was making progress. By morning, at least, I'd have a clean shirt to put on.

"So this is it," I said to myself. "I've finally landed *somewhere*." Though I wasn't sure it was anywhere I wanted to stay for long. I didn't think the Buicks would be found in a place like this. I had always imagined them living in a beautiful, elegant home with housekeepers and gardeners and plenty of everything.

Lila was nice and the rates were reasonable, but the place itself was beginning to crumble around the edges. I gave the dryer a rest, lay down on the bed and stared at the water stains on the ceiling. One looked like Uncle Onofrio's nose, another like the back end of a school bus.

The room was spare and badly decorated. A strange odor emanated from the bathroom. There were no curtains on the windows. I pulled a cheap nylon blanket around me and felt a pang of fear. I was a stranger. No one knew me here. If anything happened, if one of Mim's predictions *did* come true and Lila's Motor Lodge burned to the ground before dawn, no one would even miss me, because I wasn't supposed to be alive. A month before, this idea would have been appealing, but not now, because it was no longer just an idea. Now it was true. I was anonymous. I had a new name, one shirt and one pair of pants. I should have felt free, but I just felt scared.

"Things aren't always as they appear," a voice called out from the bathroom.

I sat up and drew the blanket to my chin. My heart jumped into my throat. The water was running in the shower and out of a cloud of steam, Rhodi appeared. She had on a red satin bathrobe and a towel wrapped around her head.

"Oh, my God, Rhodi. You scared me."

"I just love a good hot shower, Lucy. Did you try it yet? It isn't bad."

I nodded. "I didn't stay in very long. I wasn't sure

what other life-forms might be growing in there," I said.

Rhodi sat down on the edge of the bed and looked around. It was Rhodi, all right. No doubt about it. She removed the towel from her head, revealing an exotic cornucopia of kiwis and fresh star fruit.

"Nice hairdo, Rhodi."

"Why, thank you, dear. It's awfully hard to find good star fruit this time of year. They're just coming into season."

I nodded. "Well," I said, gesturing to the decor. "What do you think?"

Rhodi paused for a moment and looked around.

"The roach motel," we said together, and laughed. That's what my great-aunts called any place we passed on the road that didn't resemble the Ritz-Carlton.

"I think they'd be right about this one, though, don't you?" I said.

Rhodi just smiled and picked up an ashtray. "It's the perfect place."

"Perfect?" That was not the word I would have chosen.

Rhodi fiddled with something in her pocket. She pulled out a creamy white flower and bobby-pinned it to the side of her head, just below a plump kiwi.

"It's a gardenia," she said, reaching up and tenderly touching the soft petals. "In honor of your new town."

"It's not my town, Rhodi."

Rhodi gave a mischievous grin, stood up and walked around the room.

"You could put a plant here," she said, pointing to the nightstand. "And maybe Lila—that's her name, isn't it?—will let you make some curtains for this window."

"What are you talking about, Rhodi? I'm not staying. I really don't think I'll find the Buicks here, do you?"

"Once you pick a sign, Lucy, you should at least give it a chance." I started to protest, but she placed her hand on my shoulder and pushed me down under the blanket.

"Time for you to go to sleep now, Lucy. It's long past midnight. Things always seem darkest before the dawn. You need your beauty rest. You're going to explore Gardenia tomorrow."

I didn't have the strength to argue with her. I did as she said. I lay down and Rhodi tucked me in and brushed my forehead with the palm of her hand the way she'd done a hundred times since I'd known her.

"Will you stay with me tonight, Rhodi?"

"Ti amo, bambina," she whispered, placing her gardenia on the nightstand and turning out the light.

CHAPTER EIGHT

TAP. TAP. TAP TAP. TAP. "Crickets in the field. Crickets in the field."

A thin voice and the tapping of a hammer woke me. The sun was up, shining through the curtainless window. Rhodi was gone, but her gardenia remained on the nightstand looking as if she'd just picked it.

"Crickets in the wind. Singing. Crickets singing." The thin voice grew in volume. I got up, wrapped myself in the bedsheet and slowly approached the window from the side. Putting my back against the wall, I peered around the corner.

A small man in a long black robe was crouched close to the ground, pounding away at something with a hammer. He paused every few strokes to catch his breath. I watched him for several minutes, trying to figure out what he was doing. Finally he stopped and cocked his head in my direction.

"It's better to stand in sunlight than remain in shadow," he said.

Startled, I flattened myself against the wall, pulling the sheet tighter around me. How could he have possibly heard me over the racket he was making? Or seen me? No more than a wisp of my hair could have fallen into view. I backed away from the window, grabbed my damp shirt and pulled it over my head. I jumped into my pants and ran my fingers through my hair to work out the snarls. My hair is long and thick and when not combed for even one day becomes frizzy and completely impossible to tame. I divided it into pigtails and tied them into a knot at the back of my head.

I emerged into the sunlight, shading my eyes, and walked quietly around the little man. He stopped hammering. He was old. Very old. A very old Asian man with a long thin scar running down his left cheek.

"What are you doing?" I asked.

He smiled serenely and swung the hammer again, striking the cement walkway. The blow passed through his body like a jolt of electricity, leaving him a bit shaken.

"I love to hammer," he replied, gesturing with a crooked finger for me to kneel down beside him. He smelled of peppermint candy and incense.

On the cement before him were three small wooden boxes.

"What do you think these are?" he asked, holding one of the strange little structures up for me to get a closer look.

"Boxes?"

"Yes." He stood up, grabbing his knees for support, took me by the arm and slowly led me toward the window of the room next to mine. There were no curtains on this window, either. There wasn't any room for curtains. The entire windowsill was filled with little wooden boxes.

"What are they for?" I asked.

The man held himself up as tall as he could. He came only to my shoulders. "Chrysalises. Chrysalises of the *Danaus plexippus*," he said.

"Oh." This didn't help me very much. I was not like my friend Lydia, who could tell you the genus and species of every living thing on the planet. To me, the natural world was a big mystery. Birds were birds and trees were trees. I was always impressed by people who could tell the difference between a starling and a chickadee.

"You are more familiar with their common name," he assured me. "The cocoons of the monarch butterfly." Although his accent was rather heavy, he spoke slowly enough that I could understand him.

"Where do you find them?"

He waved his hand toward some distant place beyond the motor lodge. "Under the leaves."

"Really," I said, thinking about butterflies and species and Lydia. I wondered what she was doing right then. I wondered if she missed me.

"I think you have . . . other things on your mind. Bigger things than making homes for butterflies? Yes?"

"Yes," I said.

"When your mind is full, it is sometimes wise to focus on small things. Perhaps you will consider working for me."

"Working for *you*?"

He nodded and looked up at me. I had never seen eyes like his before. They weren't blue, or gray or even white. They were a combination of all three. He looked at me as if he could see me, but I knew he couldn't. His eyes were all clouded over with cataracts. Vi's had been kind of like that before she died. He must be blind or close to blind. That's why he knew I was standing at the window. His hearing was sharp to make up for his fading sight.

"That's very nice of you, Mr. . . . ?"

"Mr. Tariyoko." He bowed slightly. I bowed too, even though I knew he couldn't see me. When I straightened, I gazed into his eyes. They didn't move. I felt bold. I stared right at him. I had always wished that I could look directly into someone's face. Soak in every detail of them without feeling impolite. He must have known I was staring, but he didn't flinch or turn away. He simply gazed ahead, waiting for me to respond.

"I'm Lucy," I said.

"I'm glad to make your acquaintance, Lucy." He bowed again.

"I'm not sure how long I'll be staying here, Mr. Tariyoko. I'm just passing through, really."

"Just passing through? On your way somewhere else?"

"Yes."

He patted my hand. "Everything is on its way somewhere else," he said. There was a quality in his voice that reminded me of Rhodi. His words were kind, gentle like hers, and they left me with a feeling that everything might work out.

"What is it you need help with, Mr. Tariyoko?"

"Feeding caterpillars," he answered. I suddenly realized that Mr. Tariyoko was not snatching chrysalises from the leaves in Lila's cornfield, but collecting caterpillars.

"What do they eat?"

"Fresh milkweed and water. Like myself, they have a simple diet." Mr. Tariyoko was very slight. I couldn't imagine him being able to eat anything more than a bowl of rice.

"I've never done anything like that before. Are you sure you want *my* help?"

"I'm sure. You have sharp eyes, yes?"

"Yes."

"And a pure heart." It wasn't a question. He wasn't asking me. He was stating it as if he already knew it was true. I felt a terrible sense of guilt come over me. Deceiving a blind man. A pure heart? I wasn't so sure. I didn't feel very pure. I felt more like someone who'd just walked away from a train wreck and hadn't bothered to see if anyone else was all right.

"Can you begin this afternoon?" I thought for a moment. I didn't have anything on my schedule today except locating a toothbrush and a bar of soap.

"Sure. I'll help you as long as I'm here." He nodded and reached a hand out for one of mine. I thought he was going to ask me my last name, but he didn't. He just shook my hand and smiled.

"Hey, you two. Time for breakfast." Lila stood in the open doorway of the office. The aroma of bacon and coffee drifted out behind her.

"Coming, Lila," Mr. Tariyoko said, bending down to gather up his tools. "Fine woman," Mr. Tariyoko whispered to me as I helped him. "Good cook, too."

I had only tasted Lila's hash, but breakfast was even better. Lila had cleared away all the debris from the kitchen table to make room for the sumptuous feast she had created. Omelets, French toast, fried potatoes and freshly squeezed orange juice. I tried a little of everything. Mr. Tariyoko had a bowl of brown rice and a cup of tea.

"The smells are good this morning, Lila," he said.

"Yono, you've never eaten anything but rice and tea in this kitchen for the three years you've been with me. It's a mystery that you haven't wasted away to nothing right before my very eyes."

"I'm an old man, Lila. I don't need much." He smiled and his scar creased into a deep crevice on his cheek. I wondered about that scar. Mr. Tariyoko was dignified and serious, but the scar almost made him look like a pirate, as if he'd once led a wild and dangerous life. I was just about to ask him about it when Rufus jumped up next to me, looking for food.

"Little beggar," Lila said, shooing him back to his

bowl on the floor. "It'll only make you sick. You know what my theory is?" Lila turned to Mr. Tariyoko. "I think Rufus was a chef in ancient China in a previous life. That's what I think. Now he's come back as a dog and is nothing but a bundle of culinary frustration. What do you think, Yono?"

"It is very possible. I once had a grandmother who was a stone."

"What?" Lila and I chimed in together.

"Yes. A stone. She was a perfectly round woman. She liked to sit in the stream from the time the sun rose until it went to sleep. She sat with all the other stones and sometimes she would talk to them. We would find her there, my grandfather and I. He called her the Stone Woman. She had the same nature and disposition as a stone. It was hard to get her to laugh. Stones are very serious."

Lila giggled. "I've never heard that story before, Yono. Is it true?"

Mr. Tariyoko nodded and took a bite of rice. "I believe the soul never dies. It only changes form."

I smiled and Lila noticed.

"Is that what you believe too, Lucy?" she asked, heaping a serving of home fries onto her plate and dousing them with ketchup.

"Well . . . I never gave it a lot of thought until recently," I said. I didn't know Lila or Mr. Tariyoko well enough to confide in them that I had regular nocturnal visits from my dead relatives. "But now I think it's definitely a possibility," I added.

"I don't know, myself," Lila said, pondering. "I can see where the idea could be comforting to some folks, but for me it's downright scary."

"Why is that?" I asked.

"I've had five husbands, honey, and the thought of any one of them coming round again—even if only as a stone—well, I think I'll just stick with my old belief of heaven and hell awhile longer." We all laughed, and Rufus barked and ran around in circles. Lila passed me the plate of bacon.

"I bet when you got off the train in Gardenia, you never expected to discuss metaphysics with a couple of old coots like us, did you, Lucy?" Lila went on.

I smiled, feeling strangely content.

"No, I didn't." I thought I'd be eating with the Buicks. But this wasn't a bad way to start.

CHAPTER NINE

I SAW UNCLE ROCCO in the frozen foods section of the Gardenia Super Duper. At least it looked like Rocco from the rear. A short, stocky man with a black leather cap and thick fringe of hair sticking out over his ears stood with his back to me as I considered which of the six varieties of frozen corn Lila wanted. I opened the freezer door in an attempt to block his view of me and pretended to be invisible. At any moment, I expected a waft of musky cologne to sweep into my nostrils and Rocco's heavy hand to rest on my shoulder. But then the man laughed a high squeaky laugh, and I gathered my courage and peered out through the frosted glass of the freezer door. He turned and smiled at me. He had a kind, soft face, perhaps Indian or Pakistani. Definitely not Italian. Definitely not Rocco. I sighed with relief.

I knew I was being ridiculous. So what if Rocco *did* show up in Gardenia? What could he do, anyway? Drag me out of the store? Kidnap me? Well, okay, maybe he *could* do those things. I wouldn't put it past him to try. But if someone *were* looking for me, Rhodi would've let me know. I just needed to relax and not be so afraid that my uncles lurked around every corner. They believed Lucretia Sandoni was dead. Now I just had to believe it, too.

And yet, I imagined that even in the middle of Iowa, some old Sandoni customer was going to recognize me, point a finger at my chest and expose me as an impostor. "You're not Lucy Buick," they'd say. "You're Lucretia Sandoni. I knew you weren't dead. Hey, everybody, this is that girl from New York I was telling you about. The one who was supposed to have died in the fire. She didn't die at all, she's just a big fake."

Maybe I would continue to feel like a fake until I found the Buicks. I'd definitely been on the lookout for them since I'd arrived in Gardenia four days ago, but no one had yet emerged to fit their description. If in a few weeks there was no sign of them, I'd move on.

I studied Lila's list: six russet potatoes, one bag of red onions, a sprig of dill, one pint of vanilla ice cream, two packages of frozen corn, a box of prunes and some tacks.

"Sounds like an interesting recipe," I'd told her when she handed it to me.

She laughed. "Just put it all on my account."

I decided on a jumbo pack of sweet corn and closed the freezer door. I walked down the aisles, picking up the rest of the ingredients. As I passed shelves of newly stocked pasta, I felt a pang of homesickness for Olly's marinara sauce, but I kept walking, filling my basket as I went.

The checkout clerk was a girl about my age with long red hair and overalls. She was pretty, in a plain kind of way. I wondered if, by any chance, she might be a Buick. Some distant cousin. She was tall and broad shouldered. It was a possibility. I wish I had some kind of question I could ask people to determine if they were family. Like what size spark plug does the engine of a 1969 Buick use or how many cylinders does it run on? Until I knew for sure, maybe I needed to treat everyone as a potential family member and see what happened.

"Hi. Nice day," I said.

The girl smiled without responding and slid each item over the scanner until it beeped. "That'll be twenty-two oh four," she told me.

"I'm putting it on Lila Fortune's account," I said. The girl pulled out an index card from a small plastic box and marked down the total. She put everything in a brown paper bag.

"Have a good afternoon," she said, handing it to me.

"You, too," I said. Maybe she wasn't a Buick. She was kind of quiet. The Buicks were funny and a little on the chatty side. I'd keep look-ing. I grabbed my grocery bag and headed toward the door.

A warm breeze blew my hair around as I walked out of the Super Duper and down Main Street. It wasn't much of a main street, but it was colorful. There were striped awnings over shop doorways, a big American flag fluttered in front of the post office, and on each telephone pole were bright posters in a rainbow of colors. It looked as if a peacock had flown through town and caught its wings on each of the poles. I walked over to one poster that was flapping in the wind and pulled it off.

FOURTH OF JULY SQUARE DANCE
Saturday Night
Nine to Midnight
South Fork Grange
Bring a dessert ~ Bring a partner ~ Bring yourself
~Fireworks~
Tankford Hawling and the Chewy Chicken Band

"Lucy!" a man's voice shouted from behind me. My stomach tightened into a knot. "Lucy Buick!" Slowly I turned around.

It was Brian. The guy I'd met on the train. He ran to catch up with me.

"Brian McNeil," he said, smiling, his wild hair blowing in the breeze.

"I remember."

"What are you doing here?"

"I'm just picking up a few groceries," I said, looking down at the bag in my arms.

"Yes, I can see that. I mean, what are you doing in Gardenia?"

"Oh . . . I was tired of the train, so I got off."

"Just like that?"

"Just like that."

"I thought you were going to California where there aren't any tornadoes."

I shrugged. "I decided Iowa might be more interesting."

He smiled. "You're right. Iowa is much more interesting, especially now that you're here."

I felt myself begin to blush. I blushed easily and I hated it. Sometimes I could stop it if I thought about other things. I learned early on in the Sandoni family not to reveal my feelings if at all possible. They could always be used against you later on. Right now, however, I couldn't seem to help myself. All I could think about was Brian standing there smiling at me, which made me blush even more.

"Well, I better get going," I said. "Lila will be waiting for me."

"You're staying out at Lila's?"

I nodded. "You know Lila?"

"I've known Lila Fortune all my life."

"Really?" I don't know why this surprised me. After all, this was Brian's town, not mine.

"I'm headed out that way. I could give you a lift if you're walking."

"Thank you, but I'd rather walk. I made a promise to myself that if I ever got off that train, I wouldn't sit down for a week."

"I understand. I spend a lot of time on the road. It's nice to walk when you can. Looks like you have some dancing on your mind, though," he said, taking the flyer from my hand.

I shook my head. "I have two left feet."

He looked down at my feet and studied them for a minute. "They look pretty normal to me."

"I mean I can't dance."

"I don't believe people when they say they can't dance. Everybody can dance if the music is good enough. And the music at the Fourth of July dance is the best. Everyone in town will be there. You can't miss it."

"Everybody?" I said. If everyone was attending, maybe the Buicks would show up, too.

"Well, everybody but me, possibly. I'm headed to Kansas to check out some developing weather. But I might make it back in time. Will you save me a dance if I do?"

I nodded. "Only if I can get my two left feet there," I said, beginning to move in the direction of Lila's.

He laughed. "Okay, Lucy Buick, I won't hold you up any longer."

"Nice to see you again, Brian."

"Same here. Hey, now that you live in Iowa, maybe we can go looking for tornadoes together someday."

"Maybe." I smiled and walked east toward the River Road and Lila's.

The bag of groceries grew heavier as I climbed the driveway to the motor lodge. My arms were tired but the walk had been a good idea. And it had been nice running into Brian. I liked talking to him, even if he made me nervous.

I stopped in front of Mr. Tariyoko's windowsill and rested the bag on the ledge and let my arms relax. I counted the wooden boxes as I stood there catching my breath. Five in a row with at least three chrysalises in each one. I wondered what it looked like from inside a chrysalis. Was the world all dreamy and shadowy? Was it tight and restrictive? Were those little caterpillars just dying to get out and try out their wings? Or were they glad to be safe and sound in their small world? I envied them. Envied them for being able to spin a home and climb inside and emerge entirely new. It would require a lot more work on my part and take me longer than six weeks to become Lucy Buick.

"Miss Lucy?" I jumped. Mr. Tariyoko was standing beside me.

"Oh, Mr. Tariyoko." He was so quiet that I never knew he was around until he was right next to me. It could be unsettling. Almost as if he were from another world. He reminded me of pictures of Tibetan lamas I'd seen in books. The skin on his hands was as thin as tracing paper and the veins at his temples stood out like bulging blue rivers. There was something fragile and indestructible about him at the same time.

"I want to show you something," Mr. Tariyoko said, beckoning me with his finger. "After you give Lila her supplies." He must have heard me adjust the bag of groceries. He didn't miss a thing. I took the bag to Lila's kitchen and put away the frozen corn, then followed Mr. Tariyoko out to the cornfield.

Mr. Tariyoko was wearing his simple black robe and didn't speak at all until we reached the edge of the field.

"You have been in a cornfield before?" he asked.

"No. There weren't any in the town where I grew up. Mostly factories and parking lots."

He nodded. "Now the corn is small," he continued, "but it will grow above your head before the summer ends. In Okinawa, Japan, where I lived as a boy, there were no cornfields. There were sugarcane fields. Once, I became lost in a sugar field for two days until my mother found me. Cornfields in Iowa are not different from sugar fields. When this corn grows above your head, it is easy to lose your way." I looked out over the long rows of corn, trying to imagine the stalks towering above me and extending for miles in every direction.

"My grandfather, Mishito, told me the secret of never getting lost in a sugar field. I will tell you." He bent his head to mine and whispered, "You must *want* to get lost. Not care if you ever get out. That is the way. The quicker you work at being lost, the quicker you will get out." It seemed like a strange theory to me, but I was used to strange theories. I had lived with Rhodi, after all.

Mr. Tariyoko reached behind the leaf of a milkweed bush and brushed a brown caterpillar into my hand. For some reason, it had never occurred to me that I'd have to handle the little things. I had a very strong desire to fling it onto the ground and scream. In my past life, I had been a city girl and never picked up anything slimier than a wad of chewing gum. It was all I could do to stand there and let the creature ooze its way across my palm. I held it as far away from me as possible. I was glad that Mr. Tariyoko couldn't see my face.

I knew he loved these insects as much as he loved hammering their wooden boxes together. For his sake, I'd try to imagine that I was holding the finished product—a beautiful monarch.

"Caterpillars and cornfields are the same," he said, taking the caterpillar from my hand and putting it in his own. I wiped my hand on the back of my pants. “You cannot go looking for them, Lucy. If you do you’ll never find any. You must come to the field with nothing on your mind but a desire for beauty. Then you’ll find everything. Even things you never thought you’d find.”

CHAPTER TEN

I FOUND RHODI SITTING atop a stack of tires out behind Lila's Dumpster. It was Friday evening, July third, Rhodi's birthday. She was wearing a colorful sari and a red floral scarf on her head. In her hand, she carried a small cake with a tall white candle in it.

"Happy birthday, Rhodi!" I said, hopping up on the tires next to her and giving her a kiss on the cheek.

"Why, thank you, dear."

"Just one candle?"

"It's my first birthday on the other side."

"I didn't know they celebrated birthdays there."

"They don't. At least, not like this. The cake is for you, Lucy. Make a wish, dear."

I wished to find the Buicks, of course, and I blew out the candle.

Rhodi cut the tiny cake into two equal pieces and handed one to me. I'd never eaten food from the other side. I was expecting something strange and unusual, but the chocolate with orange cream-cheese frosting and little heart-shaped red hots all along the edge tasted exactly like every birthday cake Rhodi had ever baked for me. It was good to see her.

It was almost sunset, and Rufus and I had been on our way to the cornfield for a little walk when we stumbled upon Rhodi. As always, she surprised me, but Rufus seemed unfazed. Rufus, I had found out, was not the timid creature he appeared to be in Lila's kitchen. Outdoors, he was a wild thing, dragging me behind him here and there. He was no bigger than one of the jackrabbits that darted around in the tall grass behind the motor lodge, but when excited, he was stronger than a bulldog. Tonight, though, he seemed more interested in Rhodi and her birthday cake than taking me for a walk. He jumped up on her leg.

"Cute little thing," Rhodi said, picking him up and letting him lick the icing from her fingers.

"He can *see* you?" I asked, amazed. Maybe Rhodi wasn't a figment of my imagination after all. Rufus calmed right down in Rhodi's arms and stared up into her face.

"What's his name again?"

"Rufus. Rufus Alonzo Fortune."

"Oh, my goodness," Rhodi said, combing her fingers through his long fur. "Quite an illustrious name for a pip-squeak." Rufus barked, or rather, squeaked and licked Rhodi's face.

"You should have had a dog when you were young, Lucy. I don't know why we never bought one for you."

"I do. It was because of Hy. She thought they carried diseases, remember?"

Rhodi laughed. "Speaking of the queen bee herself, that's why I'm here. The sisters are on a rampage; worried I'm leading you astray. Just wanted to warn you, dear. They might show up when you least expect them."

"Thanks, Rhodi. I'm kind of getting used to people just popping up out of nowhere."

"Any luck with the Buicks?" Rhodi asked.

"No, not yet. Why? Do you know something?"

Rhodi shrugged and changed the subject. She pulled an old *National Geographic* out from under her sari, took a pair of scissors from her pocket and began cutting out photos. "I always wanted to go to India," she said, holding up a picture of a woman carrying a basket of fruit on her head. "I somehow think I would have fit in well there, don't you? If you could go to Mumbai or New Delhi, which would you choose?"

"I can't say, Rhodi. I've never been to either."

Rhodi scratched the tip of her nose. "Maybe New Delhi," she said thoughtfully.

"Are you planning a trip?"

"Oh, maybe a small excursion. I'd like to ride on an elephant."

"Can you just go anywhere you want, Rhodi?"

"Of course, dear. It's no different than in life. Possibly a bit more expeditious. And I don't get motion sickness anymore like I used to."

Expeditious? *Illustrious*? I noticed that Rhodi's vocabulary had become more sophisticated since her death.

"Is that the only reason you came, Rhodi, to warn me about the aunts?"

"Yes, and to make sure you're settling in all right."

"I am. I have a job already."

"Working with that sweet Korean man."

"He's Japanese, Rhodi."

"Sorry, dear, I'm just terrible with nationalities these days. Hard for me to see the differences in people the way I used to. Color of skin, features, it goes right by me. Where I come from appearance doesn't mean very much."

"What's it like where you come from, Rhodi?"

"It's not really a place, dear. It's more of a state."

"I don't understand."

"You will one day." Rhodi closed her magazine and hopped down off the stack of tires. "I have to go now. Goodbye, Lucy dear, and goodbye, Rufus Fortune." She whispered something in his ear, patted him on the head and put him gently on the ground. Then she was gone. Rufus barked and jumped into the air, confused by her sudden disappearance.

"What's she up to, Rufus?" I asked him, picking up his leash. But he wouldn't tell me. He just sprinted for the cornfield, dragging me behind him.

"You need something pretty to wear, Lucy," Lila insisted over tapioca pudding and lemon cookies that night at dinner. "You need to expand your wardrobe, honey. I don't mean to be bossy and I'm not exactly what you'd call a fashion queen myself, but—"

"Now, Lila," Jimmy Harlow interjected, "you're a fine dresser and a handsome woman to boot."

"Thank you, Jimmy," Lila said, dismissing his compliment.

Jimmy Harlow was the local undertaker and a regular guest, I was told, at Lila's for Friday night dinner. He was a tall, thin man with a serious face. If I could think of one word to describe Jimmy, it would be *earnest*. He was an *earnest* person. The kind who would carry your deepest darkest secret to the grave, which I guess was a good quality in his particular profession. It was also evident that Jimmy had a very earnest crush on Lila. He complimented her on everything: her cooking, her clothes, her hairstyle. But Lila just seemed to brush his attention aside.

"Pass the chicken, please?" Jimmy asked me. I passed him the platter of Lila's crispy fried chicken and looked around the table. There was an interesting mix of dinner guests. Aside from Jimmy, Lila and me, there was Mr. Tariyoko, and Nell, a lady trucker on her way to Columbus, Ohio, and Rufus, who had suddenly developed a cold.

Sheewww, Rufus sneezed.

"Jimmy, will you wipe his nose, please?" Lila asked, handing him a paper napkin.

Jimmy reached down and wiped Rufus's whole face, then threw the napkin into the trash pail behind him.

"Rufus, where did you get that cold?" Lila asked. "You were fine an hour ago." Rufus whined and looked away.

"I didn't think dogs got colds," said Jimmy.

"Of course they do." Nell spoke up. "My Pekinese gets one every fall when the weather changes. She had bronchitis last November and I had to give her antibiotics."

Rufus sneezed again and wandered over to Lila.

"Maybe he has an allergy," Lila suggested as she picked him up and wiped his nose with a tissue. She put him back onto the floor. "Maybe he's allergic to green beans." She held a bean down to Rufus. He ate it and didn't sneeze.

I had my own theories about Rufus's cold that had nothing to do with the changing weather or any green vegetable. It was Rhodi. Since she'd whispered in Rufus's ear, he'd been acting out of character, chasing his tail all the way home from our walk, and now this runny nose. Maybe it was just coincidence, but I had a strange feeling that Rhodi might be trying to entice Rufus to join her in some kind of scheme.

"The plain fact, Lucy," Lila said, coming back to her original conversation, "is that I refuse to be seen with you at any square dance if you wear those pants."

I'd been wearing the same pants *and* shirt for the past week. I'd washed them twice but they were looking dingy, and my pants had a rip in the back pocket where I'd snagged them on a raspberry bush. I didn't feel self-conscious around any of my fellow dinner companions, for obvious reasons. Mr. Tariyoko had worn the same black robe since the day I met him and couldn't see me anyway. Nell looked as if she hadn't showered in a few days. Lila wasn't exactly a fashion plate. Rufus didn't count. As for Jimmy . . . well, he was used to seeing people in all states, if you know what I mean. But for a dance, especially a dance where the Buicks might show up, I agreed that I needed something nice to wear.

Even when I'd had the opportunity to change my clothes on a daily basis back in Hamlin, though, my wardrobe had never varied much. In fact, I was so used to wearing plain clothes, I never considered any other kind.

"The Sandoni women do not attract attention to themselves," Mim used to say. "Their own natural beauty speaks for itself." From the time I was twelve, my entire wardrobe had been dominated by the color beige. Even my underwear was beige. Though Sandoni Brothers also produced a limited line of beautiful silk lingerie, I was never allowed to wear any of it. No lacy bras or pink satin teddies. There were plenty of panty hose to choose from, of course. But I refused to wear them. And I refused to wear black, the only color my great-aunts ever wore. I settled on a neutral wardrobe. Beige. Beige was the perfect color for blending in. After Rhodi died, I used to think that if I wore beige, I could disappear from my uncles' radar screen long enough to have some kind of life, but it never worked. I could have dressed up as a tree and stood in the backyard with all the other trees, and Uncle Frank still would have come out to get me when it was time to do the dishes.

"I'm not saying you should wear something fancy, Lucy. Just something pretty and colorful," Lila went on. "If you're going, that is?"

I did want to go. Since meeting Brian in town, and taping the flyer to the mirror in my bathroom, I'd been thinking about the dance. Brian might be there, and maybe *they* would be there, too. If I didn't go, I'd never know, but I was almost afraid to find out. I'd been waiting so long to meet them. My search could be over just like that or merely beginning. I wasn't sure which thought frightened me more.

"I'll go," I said quietly. "And I guess I'll be doing some last-minute stopping tomorrow." Lila smiled and Rufus gave a satisfied sneeze.

The next morning, Lila dropped me off in front of Grace's on her way to take Rufus to the vet. Before she pulled away from the curb, she made me promise that I would at least consider a bright color. I told her I'd try.

Grace's was a sweet little consignment shop, packed with an eclectic combination of styles from the 1940s on up. I browsed the racks for several minutes before choosing a yellow shirt with orange piping on the sleeves, a red skirt and a bright purple scarf.

Mrs. Newton, who owned Grace's, was a tiny woman with a Southern accent.

"Now, you just go right in there, darlin', and try on anything that tickles your fancy. I'm just gonna pop out for a few minutes to do an errand. Take in as many clothes as you like." This was very trusting of Mrs. Newton, as well as a bit overwhelming. Never having to decide what colors to wear had kept my life rather simple. Beige went with anything and everything, and best of all, it went with itself, which meant I never had to worry about matching. The world of color was far more complicated and intimidating.

Mrs. Newton "popped" out of the shop and I loaded up my arms with more shirts, skirts and dresses, which I lugged into the fitting room.

"If you must, put on the white blouse, dear, then try on those colorful skirts," a voice said as I pulled the heavy green curtain across for privacy. I looked up, expecting to see Mrs. Newton in the doorway, but she wasn't there. It was Hy. She was sitting on the little bench in the dressing room accompanied by Vi, Mim and Olly. Because of Rhodi's warning, I was not completely surprised. At least Mrs. Newton had left the shop and wouldn't hear me talking to myself in the dressing room.

"You need help, dear," Vi said, standing up and pulling a blue dress from the hook. "Try something basic first. Just one color."

"No, no, Vi," Olly interrupted. "The whole point is for Lucretia to experiment with a variety of colors." I looked at Olly as if she had grown three heads.

"Well, dear, that is why you're here, isn't it? To find something pretty to wear to the dance? To fit in a little more, even though . . ."

"Even though what?" I said.

"Nothing, Lucretia."

"Come on, Olly, what were you going to say?"

"I was just going to say even though this isn't your home."

"Olly!" Hy said. "You promised."

Olly sighed. "I was just trying to help. We're all trying to help you, Lucretia."

"You are?" It was hard to believe.

"Olly's right," Hy interjected. "We've had a little talk with our *other* sister and we've come to the conclusion—"

Vi nudged Hy in the ribs. "We've come to a general understanding that if you are determined to make a go of it in this place—" Hy went on.

"Gardenia," Mim chimed in.

"Gardenia," Hy repeated. "We should put our own desires aside and see if we can't help you."

"Really?"

"Yes, dear, of course. Now, here, try the white blouse with this skirt." She held out a long peasant skirt. "We won't look." My great-aunts turned their backs and studied the wallpaper. I don't think any of them had ever been in a dressing room before. They had always ordered their black dresses from Benson's mail-order catalog and all their undergarments had come directly from the factory.

I smiled to myself. They were trying. Just getting them all to agree on one course of action must have taken all Rhodi's patience.

I put on the peasant skirt with the white blouse and told them it was safe to turn around.

"Okay, what do you think?" My great-aunts smiled and offered their conflicting opinions.

"Too small."

"Too tight."

"Too dark."

"Too revealing!"

Over the next forty minutes, I tried on sixteen

separate outfits, none of which they could agree on. But, at least, by the time Mrs. Newton returned from her errands, I had decided what *I* wanted. With a feeling of great accomplishment, I emerged (auntless) from the dressing room with a very nice outfit that wasn't beige, that matched, and that none of my great-aunts liked. I knew I was on the right track.

CHAPTER ELEVEN

THE SOUTH FORK GRANGE SAT on the very edge of Gardenia. It was an old wooden structure with a stage and a big dance floor. It smelled of wax and chewing gum and coffee. It also smelled of human beings—a mixture of sweet and sweaty. The old building was packed with all varieties of them by the time Lila and Mr. Tariyoko and I arrived.

Before leaving the motor lodge, I'd confessed to Lila that I was nervous being in a room full of people I didn't know, but she assured me that the crowd would be so thick I could blend in if I wanted to. Only this time I wouldn't blend in because of the way I was dressed. Thanks to Lila.

I had decided on a rose-colored skirt, black cowboy boots, a white silk shirt and a brown suede vest. Lila had braided my hair and let me borrow a little lipstick and perfume. She said I looked beautiful, but I felt like an impostor. Someone was sure to see through the exterior and know that this wasn't me. I was playing a part. Like Cinderella, I'd change back into the beige girl by midnight and disappear again.

"Punch, anyone?" Jimmy asked as he appeared out of the crowd, balancing two paper cups in one hand, both brimming over with a dark sweet-looking liquid. He passed one to Mr. Tariyoko and the other to me.

"Don't I get any?" Lila said, pouting.

"Not until you dance with me." Jimmy offered his arm. Lila hesitated for a second, then took it.

"Just one dance, Jimmy. That's all I have in me." Lila looked tired. She'd been trying to nurse Rufus back to health with little success. Even the vet couldn't determine what was wrong with him. Poor Rufus had only gotten worse and Lila, afraid to leave him home alone, had brought him to the dance. She was almost positive that he had a fever now. "Lucy, will you take Rufus for me?"

"Sure, Lila." I boosted Rufus into my arms. His little body felt hot.

"I think I know what is wrong with Mr. Rufus," Mr. Tariyoko said as he and I sat down on folding chairs that had been set up to the side.

"You do?"

"I think he wants to say something but doesn't know how." Mr. Tariyoko patted the top of Rufus's furry head. "I believe he wants our attention on some matter."

"It could be." Rufus buried his face in the crook of my arm and whined. Mr. Tariyoko and I sat back and took in the scene before us and talked of the progress of the butterflies. Within a few weeks, Mr. Tariyoko assured me, we would see the first of them emerge from their chrysalises. For the short time I had known him, my butterfly-loving neighbor had always appeared to be a very calm and orderly kind of person, but tonight he seemed excited and barely able to sit still in his chair. His foot kept tapping on the floor.

"Do you want to dance, Mr. Tariyoko?" I asked.

He smiled. "No thank you, Lucy. I like to sit and listen."

I looked toward the musicians. A large man with a heavy red beard was onstage, holding a beautiful fiddle under his chin, the bow flying across the strings.

He played so effortlessly, it seemed as if the fiddle itself were singing. The sweet notes spread through the crowded hall, and like Mr. Tariyoko, I was caught up in the sound. It brought me back to those moments when I'd held my own violin in a similar fashion.

Sometimes, when I was practicing for a lesson, the music just flowed out of me and I almost forgot that I was playing at all. I felt as if I could lift the bow off the strings and the violin would continue without me. I missed that feeling. I missed my violin. I knew exactly where I had left it—in its case at the foot of my bed back on Connelly Street. I wished I had it with me right then.

I gazed out at the dancers, feeling a little lonely. Everyone seemed to have a partner and know each other. Little children danced with old folks; young couples swung each other around, laughing. Maybe Olly was right. All these people were part of a world I knew nothing about.

"Are you looking for someone in particular, Lucy?"

Mr. Tariyoko's question startled me. I'd forgotten that be could see with things other than his eyes. "Not really. I was just hoping I might recognize someone, that's all."

"Who?"

"Some people I've been looking for."

"And they live here . . . in Gardenia?"

"I'm not sure, Mr. Tariyoko. Maybe."

"I hope you find them."

"So do I." Rufus squirmed in my arms and started sneezing. People nearby turned in our direction. Then Rufus began barking. I looked around for Lila, thinking she might be coming toward us, but there was no sign of her.

"Shhh, Rufus." I tried to quiet him. "It's all right. Lila will be back soon." I wished I could wipe his nose, which was about to drip on my skirt, but Lila hadn't left me a tissue and I wasn't going to forfeit my new clean sleeve for that purpose. I held him out away from me so that if the mucus dripped, it would do so onto the floor.

"Lucy?"

I looked up, still holding Rufus at a distance. A man in a jean jacket stood directly in front of me. The lights from the stage blocked his face from view.

"It's me, Brian," he said, stepping out of the spots. For a moment I'd thought my conversation with Mr. Tariyoko had conjured up a Buick. I let out a sigh.

"Hi, Brian." I put Rufus down on the floor.

"So you came," he said.

"I did. Lila convinced me." Brian looked very handsome in a clean white shirt, and with his wild hair combed down. But as glad as I was to see him, my stomach suddenly felt queasy. Maybe I was catching Rufus's cold.

"And is this gentleman your escort?" he asked, referring to Mr. Tariyoko.

"We're keeping each other company. Brian, this is Mr. Tariyoko. He's my neighbor," I said, introducing them.

"He's *my* neighbor too," Brian said, putting a hand on Mr. Tariyoko's shoulder. "How are you, Mr. T.?"

"Very well, Brian. I hope you come by Lila's soon."

"I will. There are a lot of reasons to stop by." He turned to me. "Dance?" he asked.

"I'll take Rufus for you, Lucy." Mr. Tariyoko reached out his hands.

"Are you sure?"

"Oh, yes." I picked up Rufus and passed him to Mr. Tariyoko. His nose was moist, but it wasn't dripping anymore. "Rufus and I are going to have a little talk about his health," Mr. Tariyoko said as he placed Rufus in his lap. No doubt Rhodi would figure prominently in the conversation. Brian took my hand and I stood up.

"I never would have seen you in this sea of people if Rufus hadn't barked when he did," Brian said.

"I was just thinking the same thing."

Brian and I danced to six songs in a row without

having a chance to say much to each other, because I was always getting twirled away from him and changing partners. I surprised myself. I was definitely holding my own out there.

"Hey, you're not bad," Brian said. "I think you have one left foot now and one right foot, just like everybody else. How did that happen?"

I smiled. "Must be from living in Iowa."

"Must be," he said, swinging me around. Brian was wild on the dance floor, and funny, too. He kept twirling me around even after the music stopped and the fiddler announced the next song.

"Slow dance, folks," the fiddler said in a deep baritone. "Grab your sweetheart." He picked up his fiddle and winked at us. Brian waved.

"That's my cousin Small."

"Small?"

"Yeah, you know. He's so big, it'd be kind of redundant to call him by his real name."

"Which is?"

"Tank. Tankford Hawling. That's his real name. He's my cousin on my mother's side. Most of my family is here tonight." He pointed to a tall, pretty blond woman across the hall from us. "That's my mother over there. And that's my dad, talking to Mr. T. I have a whole slew of siblings around as well. Most of the kids you see with wild hair are McNeils." The music started and Brian put his hand on my waist, pulling me closer. I tried to act cool, but my stomach was going crazy. Brian had a strange effect on me. Maybe he was electrically charged from running into too many storms. Whatever it was, I found that the only thing that helped me stay calm was keeping my focus on the music.

"I could listen to your cousin play all night long," I said over Brian's shoulder.

"So you like fiddle music?"

I nodded. "Yes. I play the fiddle . . . violin, actually. There aren't many fiddle players where I come from."

"And where is it that you come from? I can't recall you telling me."

"Probably because I didn't." We passed by Lila and Jimmy. Lila raised her eyebrows and smiled at me. "I'm from New York. Upstate New York."

"What do they play in upstate New York, then? Classical violin?"

"Something like that. But I taught myself some folk music and my violin teacher played fiddle. I made her teach me everything she knew. It's my favorite kind of music."

"You should be up there right now then, Lucy, playing us a tune."

I shook my head. "I don't play like your cousin Small does."

"Of course you don't, you play like you."

When the song ended, Brian let go of me and jumped onto the stage and whispered in Tank's ear. My heart started thumping in my chest. Tank smiled and nodded and Brian reached down for my hand. I took it and he pulled me up.

"Well, little lady, my cousin here says you can really set the wood on fire," Small said.

I didn't know what to say. I was terrified. I had a very strong urge to run away. It was worse than leaving Hamlin, even. At least that had been under cover of night. I couldn't hide anywhere here—and I wanted to badly. I knew how to do that. I'd been hiding most of my life. But I was no longer beige and Brian was waiting and so was Tank.

He handed me his beautiful fiddle. "Play us something sweet."

"Okay," I said, slowly taking the instrument from him as if in a dream. I couldn't think of one song I'd ever played. My mind was a complete blank. I stood there frozen while the band settled themselves for another song. The banjo player looked over at me for direction.

"Do you know 'The Roseville Fair'?" I finally whispered. It was the first thing that came to me. I could feel that song inside me somewhere. He nodded.

Tank got up to the microphone. "My cousin Brian

has brought us some new talent tonight. A young lady from the East who's going to serenade us. I'd like to introduce *Lucy* . . . ," he said, placing his big hand on my shoulder and giving me a quizzical look.

"Buick," I whispered.

"Lucy Buick." My name echoed through the hall. Everyone clapped.

"Whooooh, Lucy!" It was Lila cheering from the back of the hall. I couldn't look out at the crowd or I knew I would be sick, so I simply put my bow on the strings.

As I played the first note, couples came together for another slow dance. My terror slowly began to leave me. I hadn't forgotten how to play after all. It was the same amazing feeling standing on the stage as in my room at home. Even if I didn't belong in Gardenia, while I played, I belonged to the music.

When the song ended, I handed the fiddle to Tank. He patted me on the back. "Nice going, little lady. Come to practice next week."

"Really?"

"You betcha. We can use that kind of talent. Every Thursday. Here. Seven o'clock."

"Okay," I said, feeling stunned.

"Lucy, honey, I didn't know you could play like that," Lila said, helping me down from the stage.

"Me either," I said, catching my breath. Brian took my hand.

"You were incredible," he whispered, keeping his eyes on me.

"And you, Brian McNeil, how long have you known my Lucy?" Lila said teasingly as we all walked toward the refreshment table.

"I didn't know she was *your* Lucy." Brian gave Lila a hug. "We met on the train."

"Lucy never mentioned it," she said, smiling at me. "And where have you been that you're riding on trains these days?"

"All over," Brian said.

"Do you know, Lucy, that when this fellow was little he'd come over to my house every morning to sell me eggs. And now I'm lucky if I catch a glimpse of him once a year."

"Small world," I said. I felt that old familiar jab of loneliness return, and longing for family, as I watched Lila and Brian. I wanted so much to feel connected and wondered if it would ever happen. I hadn't seen anyone tonight who looked like a Buick, No one had suddenly rushed out of the crowd to claim me . . . except Lila.

"Well, that was the highlight of my evening," Lila said. She gave me a hug. "Lucy, you are just full of surprises." Jimmy put Lila's sweater over her shoulders.

"Are you leaving?" I asked.

"Jimmy and I are going to take Yono and Rufus home. I want to leave with your music in my ears. Besides, I'm pretty tuckered out and Rufus hates fireworks. He needs his rest. Do you want to come with us?"

"I'll take Lucy home if she wants to stay longer," Brian interjected.

"Where are the fireworks?" I asked.

"Out back by the river," Brian said. "Just in case."

"In case of what?"

"In case Charlie Bemus lights the wrong fuse and the fire department can't get here on time."

"I thought the fire department was *already* here . . . dancing," Lila joked.

"Well, I guess I'll stay, if you don't mind, Lila," I said.

"Why would I mind? Have a good time, honey. And don't come home too early."

CHAPTER TWELVE

"He likes you, Lucy."

"I know, Rhodi."

"So what are you going to do?"

"Nothing."

"Seems a shame. He's very nice-looking."

"How do you know? You've never seen him."

Rhodi blushed. "I peeked out the window when he was dropping you off."

"Rhodi! Have you been spying on me?"

"No, of course not, dear. I just happened to be

here when you drove up. You look lovely, by the way. Nice outfit. Colorful."

It had been past midnight when I'd opened the door of my room to find Rhodi perched on the edge of the bed wrapped in a sari. She was playing solitaire.

"Well, he might be nice-looking, Rhodi, but he chases tornadoes and he's a crazy dancer. Somehow I think there might be a sign there."

"Yes," Rhodi said thoughtfully. "I think there might be."

"He's not a Buick, that's for sure." I kicked off my boots and lay down on the bed beside her.

"How do you know?"

"Because I have a feeling about the Buicks and I just don't have that feeling around Brian."

Rhodi twisted up her eyebrows and stared at me. "I don't know what feeling you mean, dear."

"Well, I just always had this feeling that I'd know when I met the Buicks. There'd be some strong sign. I'd feel all warm inside and happy and right . . . in a certain way. I'd feel relaxed."

"And you don't feel relaxed around Brian?"

"Not exactly." Contrary to my idea that fresh air and fireworks would take my mind off my churning stomach, it had only gotten worse. As Brian and I sat in his truck wrapped in an old wool blanket and watched the twenty-minute pyrotechnical display, I kept praying that I'd make it through the evening without being ill. Without passing out, which almost happened when Brian pulled me close to him. I had to get out of the truck and walk around. I'm sure he thought I was crazy.

"No. I think it's safe to say that I do not feel relaxed around Brian McNeil."

"Love can be unsettling."

"Love? I'm not in love, Rhodi. I barely know Brian."

"Your stomach is in love."

I sat up. "How do you know about my stomach?"

She shrugged. "I was in love once and I couldn't eat for weeks. Could hardly even stand up straight. Your aunt Vi was the same way."

"I never knew you were in love. Who with?"

"Oh, no one you knew, dear. It was a long time ago. I was only sixteen or seventeen." She looked down at her hands. "It wasn't my destiny to marry, Lucy, and have that kind of life."

I felt an old sadness come over me whenever Rhodi spoke like that. It reminded me of times back in Hamlin when the kids on Connelly Street would make fun of her. They teased her for wearing fruit in her hair. They threw things at her. Called her names. Once, I remember standing behind the lilac bush in our front yard watching Rhodi walk by them all with her head held high, tomato juice and rotten apple bits sticking to the back of her dress. I thought my heart would break in two. I wished I could make things right for Rhodi—give her a normal face, a normal life. I never wanted Rhodi to be any different for my sake. But for her sake . . . well . . . sometimes I just wished.

"There's no need to rush anything, Lucy. I'm just saying—"

"I know what you're saying, Rhodi." I was touched by her concern for my love life, but I felt rather confused. I wasn't sure if I wanted to get involved with anyone, especially since I didn't know how long I was staying in Gardenia. I couldn't let a few stomach cramps sidetrack me from my real mission of finding the Buicks.

I refluffed my pillows and lay back down. "I have to get up early tomorrow to help Mr. Tariyoko. I'm going to sleep now. Or maybe I'm already asleep and you're just a dream, Rhodi. Maybe this is all just a dream."

"There's a very fine line between life and dreams."

"Good night, Rhodi." I rolled over.

"Good night, dear."

CHAPTER THIRTEEN

A PINK CERAMIC PORCUPINE SAT on Lila's kitchen table. It was two feet high with a bright yellow ribbon tied around its neck and a note attached.

"Don't have to read the note to know who that's from, do you?" Lila asked me as she placed a big green salad on the table and sat down. I shook my head. Jimmy, I had found out, had a habit of sending Lila rare and unusual gifts. Last week he'd mailed her an ashtray in the shape of a pelican from an undertakers' convention in Omaha.

"Start in, honey. I don't think Yono's coming tonight." She passed me a bowl of cold cucumber soup. It was the perfect night for cold soup. The temperature had passed ninety degrees in Lila's kitchen. It seemed too early in the summer for a heat wave, but then again it was mid-July. The time had passed quickly. I'd been in Gardenia almost a month.

I sliced myself some of Lila's homemade bread, buttered it and fanned myself with a napkin. Lila took a cube of ice from her lemonade and rubbed it on her neck. We ate in silence. Mr. Tariyoko was absent and even though he rarely said much, it felt quieter without him. Rufus, whose fever had still not broken, was resting on Lila's bed in the other room.

"It's not a good sign," Lila told me as she shook a liberal amount of salt into her soup.

"What's not?"

She gestured with her head toward the porcupine. "The bigger the gifts, Lucy . . ."

I shrugged. "I don't understand."

"Let's just say that last year Jimmy sent me a satellite dish, and the next day he asked me to marry him."

"That's so romantic."

Lila widened her eyes. "Romantic to *you*."

"You turned him down?"

"I saved him is what I did. And the dish went back to the warehouse."

"Saved him from what?"

"Me. Lucy, I've been married five times and I've learned the hard way that I'm not the kind of woman to find lasting happiness with a man, not even if he sends me ceramic porcupines every day of my life."

"But, Lila, how do you know Jimmy wouldn't be different? He's very sweet, and anybody can tell he's in love with you. Besides, you've known him a long time, haven't you? That's always a good sign."

"I don't believe in signs. But you're right. I've known Jimmy longer than I knew all my husbands put together. But he's *too* sweet. Just the way he's taken care of Rufus since the dance. It's too good to be true. Those are the ones you have to watch out for, honey. The sweet ones will take your heart if you let them and never give it back."

"Maybe you're just afraid," I said, surprised that Lila didn't believe in signs.

Lila put down her spoon and smiled. "Maybe *you're* just afraid."

"What do you mean?"

"Brian McNeil."

"What about Brian?"

"You two looked very natural dancing together at the Grange. Brian's one of the nicest young men I know. And he's called you at least half a dozen times since then. Am I right to say that there is a bit of hesitation on your part?"

"He wants to take me out to dinner."

"And?"

"I've been too busy working for Mr. Tariyoko," I offered as an excuse.

"And going to fiddle practice." I'd been practicing the past two Thursday nights down at the Grange with Tank and the Chewy Chickens. Tank had found me an old fiddle to use. It was great to be playing again.

"Neither of those activities takes all your time, Lucy."

"I know. I just don't want to get involved with anyone right now, Lila. I came here to look for something and until I find it, I can't be distracted. I don't know how long I'm going to be here, anyway."

Lila considered this. "What are you looking for, Lucy?"

"It's a little hard to explain."

Lila nodded. "I see. Sometimes it's easier to look for something and scarier to actually find it," she said. There was a long silence. Lila passed me the salad and I refilled our water glasses. My situation was different from Lila's. She knew she belonged here. I didn't. I ran my finger along the shiny surface of the porcupine.

"So, what are you going to do about Jimmy?" I said, changing the subject.

"Well, for one thing, I'm sending back this porcupine and the ashtray and I'm going to tell Jimmy Harlow to go look for happiness somewhere else, 'cause it ain't here."

"Maybe I should tell Brian the same thing."

"No," Lila protested. "You're young. You have a whole life ahead of you."

"So do you."

"I'm fifty-two years old, Lucy. I've put in my time."

I sighed. "You and I are a lot alike, Lila. I don't want to complicate my life and neither do you. So it's settled. We'll stay away from men forever, and we'll enjoy our freedom."

Lila laughed. "We can eat hot fudge sundaes every night and grow fat and happy and never care about what we look like."

"And paint our toenails purple."

"And let our hair go gray."

"And never take a bath."

"And never brush our teeth."

"That's disgusting."

"I know." We both started laughing and woke up Rufus, who hobbled out to the kitchen, plunked himself down on the floor under the table and let out a deep sigh.

"Rufus, honey, get back to bed this instant," Lila scolded. But Rufus just lay at our feet.

"There is only one problem with our plan," I said, rubbing my foot gently along Rufus's back.

"What's that?"

"Ending up in the Land of What If."

"The Land of What If?"

"The land of what could have been. It was a place my great-aunt Rhodi always warned me about. She said if you never took any chances, you'd never know. Maybe you would have lived happily ever after instead of ending up a smelly, toothless, fat old lady."

Lila smiled. "Nobody lives happily ever after, Lucy."

"I'm going to."

"With Brian?"

"No, with the Buicks."

"Your family?"

"Yes. That's who I'm looking for . . . family."

"Isn't your great-aunt Rhodi family?"

"She died last fall."

"Oh, that's too bad, honey. She sounds like a very smart lady."

I laughed. "She'd agree with you."

"What would she tell you to do about Brian, then?" Lila winked and passed me a basket of rolls. I had the feeling she was asking for herself, too.

"Trust myself."

"Mmmm." Lila suddenly looked up and gazed over my head toward the door. For a moment I thought maybe Rhodi was standing there.

"Yono?" Lila whispered. I turned around in my chair, and Rufus got to his feet and whined. Mr. Tariyoko stood in the doorway. He stood very still with his right arm out in front of him. The light outside was fading and the kitchen was growing dim. It was difficult to see him.

"The first one," Mr. Tariyoko said, walking toward us. On the sleeve of his robe perched a monarch butterfly. I could hear Lila catch her breath. She got up and pulled out a chair for Mr. Tariyoko and the latest addition to her motor lodge. Very gingerly, Mr. Tariyoko sat down and rested his arm on the table.

"I am sorry to miss dinner," he whispered. "But I couldn't leave her."

"I thought it might be something like that," Lila whispered back.

"Can she fly yet?" I asked, moving closer. I wanted to touch her, but I didn't think I should. The monarch was fanning her delicate new wings in the warm air of the kitchen. They were as thin as tissue paper. She clung to Mr. Tariyoko's sleeve.

"Soon. I came to ask if you'd like to join me in bidding her farewell."

"Already?" I said, disappointed. "She just arrived. Why does she have to leave so quickly?"

"She's been here since midmorning. Her wings have had sufficient time to dry. Come with me." Lila scooped Rufus into her arms and the two of us abandoned our dinner. We followed Mr. Tariyoko out the back door.

The sun had set over the cornfield and the air was beginning to cool a bit. I was amazed every time I stepped outside after sunset. The smell of the countryside was incredible. Damp ground and honeysuckle scents blended together in a heady fragrance. I wished that I could collect it in a bottle and keep it for the winter. I wanted to breathe it all in.

Lila's cornfield was now up to our shoulders. In another week, it would be above my head. July was passing quickly.

"Same place as last year, Yono?" Lila asked. He nodded. Lila led us to her little sunflower garden at the edge of the cornfield. The wind was blowing to the east and the crickets were beginning to sing. We stood together, the three of us, and suddenly I felt that maybe I *had* done the right thing by getting off the train in Gardenia and following the sign to the motor lodge. If the Buicks were half as interesting as Lila and Mr. Tariyoko, everything would be fine.

"Last year, we had that six-foot-four trucker with

us, remember?" Lila said. Mr. Tariyoko nodded. Lila measured the three of us with her hand. "But this year, the prize goes to Lucy. You're the tallest, honey." Mr. Tariyoko smiled. He laid his index finger in front of the butterfly and it crawled onto it; then he held her out to me.

Slowly, the butterfly stepped onto my fingers. I could barely feel her.

"Now, Lucy, hold her up to the wind," he said. I stretched my arm up as high as it could go. The monarch fanned her wings. The sunflowers fluttered around her and then a little gust came by and she lifted off. She let go without any hesitation.

"Ooooh. I love this part," Lila said as she jumped up and down. "Look at her. Look at her go. Isn't that amazing? She's like a leaf in the wind. How can she do that?"

As I watched the monarch flutter away, I suddenly knew the answer to Lila's question.

"She's not afraid," I said, softly. "That's what it is. She trusts herself."

"And she trusts the wind," said Mr. Tariyoko.

CHAPTER FOURTEEN

"THAT'S THE CHICKEN," Brian said, pointing up to the sky.

I thought he was referring to one of the strange weather terms he'd been telling me about, like *beaver's tail* or *dust devil*, but there was an actual five-foot-tall white chicken perched on the roof of the restaurant where we were going for takeout. After my last conversation with Lila, I had decided that if I wanted her to give Jimmy a chance, I could at least accept Brian's dinner invitation.

"Dixie Chicken has the best french fries in all of Iowa," Brian informed me as we pulled into the parking lot under the feet of the giant bird.

On our short drive out of Gardenia, I had discovered that Brian was a connoisseur of fast food. He knew the best place to find chocolate shakes, fried clams and onion rings. He told me it was a result of growing up in a farm family where everything was made from scratch and where milk came directly from the cow. That sounded nice to me, but Brian disagreed.

"I always longed for junk food."

"Really?" I made a face. "I haven't had a lot of junk food myself."

"You'll love it, Lucy, won't she, Jack?" Brian's big golden retriever, Cracker Jack, sat between us. He panted and licked Brian's face. This dog was a big part of the reason I had ended up in Gardenia. I patted his head and he licked my face, too.

"Jack!" Brian scolded, pulling him away from me. "Have some manners, boy. We have a lady in the car."

"Is Jack a fast-food lover too?" I asked.

"No." Brian shook his head. "He's very particular. Aren't you, Jack? He goes mostly for squirrels."

I scrunched up my nose. "Really?"

"It's true. He catches and eats them. Has ever since he was a pup. It's very unusual for his breed, but it comes in handy sometimes when we're on the road.

He makes an exception for Dixie's fries, though." Jack whined and nudged Brian's arm with his nose. Brian opened the door and they both got out.

"We'll be right back, Lucy. Don't go anywhere."

Where would I go? I wondered. For miles in all directions there was nothing but straight flat highway and sky. The landscape of eastern Iowa was still strange to me. I was always looking for the silhouettes of buildings and church steeples to break up all that openness. But the land was what it was. Flat and sometimes rolling, but not dramatic. That was reserved for the sky. The sky here was immense and always changing. I understood how Brian could watch it all day long.

While I waited, I looked around the inside of the truck. It was by the far the messiest front seat area I had ever been in. Old food wrappers were strewn on the floor, along with soda bottles, and something that looked like a half-eaten bologna sandwich was wedged into a narrow space beneath the radio. In the backseat were stacks of old newspapers and maps of all kinds: topographic maps, weather maps, maps of Oklahoma, Kansas and Texas. I pulled out the map of Iowa, located Melrose County and traced my finger five miles north of Gardenia. Dixie Chicken was right next to a little soda stain at the intersection of Route 4 and the River Road. I had the feeling that Brian was one of those people who read maps, ate and drove all at the same time.

I placed the map back where I'd found it and pulled out an old yellowed copy of the *Chicago Tribune*. It was folded over to page sixteen, where someone had circled a story about a weather balloon in Illinois getting shot down by hunters who had mistaken it for a goose. I was just beginning to read all about it when Brian opened the car door and held up two bulging bags of food.

"That was quick!" I said.

"Wait till you see what we have for you." Cracker Jack jumped up next to me and Brian slid into the driver's seat. He opened one of the bags and pulled out a chicken wing.

"Here you go," he said. "The whole idea behind fast food is that you have to eat it while doing something else, like driving."

I smiled. My theory was correct.

Brian fed Jack a french fry and turned the key in the ignition. As we drove out of the parking lot, I bit into the chicken wing.

"What do you think?" Brian asked as he maneuvered the truck with one hand and ate a fry with the other.

"Not bad. I think the exhaust fumes really add something to the flavor."

He laughed. "The real reason I want to get on the road is to show you the clouds before it gets dark."

"Okay. Let's go." I had a few french fries and a bite or two of chicken.

"You eat like a bird, Lucy."

I shrugged. "I haven't been very hungry lately," I said. I pulled off some chicken and gave it to Jack. I wasn't going to admit that being in Brian's presence was contributing to my lack of appetite.

"We're going to drive east," Brian said, pointing straight ahead. "Away from Gardenia, toward the Melrose town line."

I hadn't driven outside of Gardenia since I'd arrived. There were so many miles between one town and the next. *It must be like this in Kansas and Oklahoma*, I thought—*only flatter*.

"Don't you ever get scared?" I asked as Brian put the truck into fourth gear.

"Scared?"

"Being so far away from a town when a big storm is coming?"

"Yep. I get scared a lot. The closer I get to the storm."

"Why do you do it, then?"

"I love it. Besides, there's nothing wrong with being scared."

"So what's it like to be out there?"

"Well, that depends on what's going on."

"Say there's a really big storm, like one of those funnels you like so much."

"Big storm, huh? Let's see. What story should we tell her, Jack?" Cracker Jack whined and licked Brian's face. "Oh, yeah. That's a good one. The Oklahoma Terror." He smiled mischievously.

I sighed. "Okay, let's hear it."

Brian settled in behind the wheel, ran one hand over Cracker Jack's head and took a deep breath. "I was following a storm system outside Tulsa, Oklahoma, about a year and a half ago," he began. "There were strong veering winds, lots of indications that a tornado would develop, maybe a relatively weak one, but then the conditions changed and it worked itself into a full-fledged twister. I should have seen it coming. The signs were all there. Anyway, by that point, I was too close to it. I couldn't turn back. And I didn't want to. There's something magnetic about a storm like that. It draws you in."

"What happened?"

"The sky turned green and the wind was full of debris; hay and sticks flying everywhere. I even saw a sneaker whirl by. I was caught right in the thick of it. Couldn't have been closer if I'd tried. I forgot all the rules. I didn't get out of the truck. I didn't find a ditch. When I saw that beast spinning toward me, I froze.

There was this incredible roaring sound and I knew that at any second the truck was going to get sucked up into the funnel and I'd be hurled into oblivion. Then this strange calm came over me and I remember thinking, 'This is what it must feel like right before you die.' "

"But you didn't."

"Nope. I was spun into the funnel. I lost my right shoe, but not my left, and I landed in Munchkin Land." He laughed.

"Seriously."

"Seriously, a huge piece of corrugated steel from somebody's roof came flying at my windshield, bounced off the hood and spun the truck around about six times. I held on to the wheel, but there was nothing I could do. And then suddenly it all stopped. The twister changed course."

"Just like that?"

He nodded. "Just like that."

"That's unbelievable."

"My mother called it a miracle."

"What do you think?"

"Felt like a miracle at the time. But that's also what tornadoes do. They change their minds at the last minute. Kind of like women." He winked at me.

We came to an intersection and Brian stopped the

truck. He turned to look at me with his incredibly blue eyes. "Did I answer your question?" he asked.

"Yes. I mean . . . everything except *why* you go out there."

"That I can't explain. I just have to go. If there's a storm, I want to be there. It's funny 'cause I used to be afraid of things when I was a kid. Afraid of something happening to my family, mostly. But other things, too, like storms and dogs and bad dreams. My grandmother, the one who made kites, used to say that she never worried about folks who felt scared because they were the ones who often took risks in life. It was all the other folks, the ones who spent their whole lives trying to stay safe, that she worried about. So I'd rather have a tornado coming at me than one at my back." He reached over Cracker Jack and pulled a map from the backseat and spread it out in front of us.

"I just want to show you where we're headed," he said, changing the subject. I followed his finger as he traced the lines from Gardenia to the little town of Melrose. "It's only about five more miles. I'm hoping to collect some data about a storm system that might be moving into this region in a couple of days." He paused and looked out through the windshield. "See that cloud? That big billowy one."

"Yeah. It's pretty."

"It is, isn't it?" He seemed pleased that I would find a cloud pretty. "Well, that pretty puff is a cumulus cloud, and that's what we're looking for. Basically, when the cumulus clouds are high enough in the sky for rain to fall, a thunderstorm is in the making. It's a little early to tell, but it could develop into a substantial storm."

"Is that what you're hoping for?"

"You bet." He put the car in drive and turned right onto a dirt road. "It gets a little rough from here on out. Hang on, you two." As the truck hit one pothole after the next, Jack and I kept bumping into each other. At one point, Jack turned and looked at me as if he were about to say something, but then he just yawned. I realized that Jack was used to rough roads. This was just part of the deal when you went looking for storms with Brian McNeil.

By the time Brian pulled the truck off to the side of the road again, the sky was darkening. He turned off the engine, got out, grabbed some instruments from the back of the truck and waved for us to follow. I could tell that he was deep in concentration. We didn't speak as we climbed a small hill to an outcropping of rocks.

"Come up here, Lucy." He gave me his hand and pulled me up next to him. We sat down on a flat rock.

Brian took notes as he searched the sky, and Cracker Jack bounded off looking for wildlife.

"May I?" I asked, pointing to Brian's binoculars.

"Absolutely," he said, handing them to me.

I held them up to my eyes and looked out over the wide expanse of open prairie. There was just enough light in the sky to see the silhouette of the grange hall below us in the distance.

"Nice view."

"Here," he said, gently guiding the binoculars a few inches to my left. "That's the Bowden Reservoir over there." I adjusted the focus until a shimmering oval of water came into view. "I used to drive over here a lot more when I was in high school."

"Is this where you brought all your girlfriends?" I couldn't help asking.

He smiled. "No, I came by myself. To think."

"I used to have a place like that, too," I said. "It was up on this ridge overlooking the town where I lived. It wasn't as nice as this, though. My view was mostly of houses and factories. But I could see everything from there. Once I even spotted my great-aunt hanging out my underwear on the clothesline in the backyard. It wasn't pretty—the town, I mean. Not like Gardenia. It was old and industrial . . . a bit run-down."

"Haml . . ."

"What?"

"Nothing."

"What were you going to say, Brian?"

"Hamlin. I was going to say Hamlin."

I stared at him. I couldn't believe I'd heard correctly. "How do you know about Hamlin?" I managed to say.

"I'm sorry, Lucy. I didn't mean to have it come out like that." He turned toward me. "I know about the fire and everything."

I looked at him, bewildered. He reluctantly pulled a crumpled piece of paper from his pocket and handed it to me. It was a page from the *New York Times*, dated June twenty-first. I uncrumpled it and scanned the headlines until I came upon the one I had only imagined until now.

GIRL DIES IN SANDONI BROTHERS BLAZE

Underneath was a picture of me.

"It's my dad," Brian explained. "He's crazy about news. He gets papers from all over the country. *Los Angeles Times*, *Chicago Tribune*, *New York Times*. He circles articles related to weather or natural phenomena for me. This was right below a piece on the winds of Long Island Sound. That's how I saw it."

I thought of all those yellowed newspapers in the back of his truck.

"How long have you known?" I whispered, letting the paper fall into my lap.

"I read this article the day I got back from my trip to Kansas. I recognized your face right away. I thought, 'Hey, that's that pretty girl from the train I sat next to who ate all my potato chips.' But I never thought I'd see you again."

I stared ahead of me toward the shimmering basin of water out on the plain. I felt naked. Exposed. And it didn't feel good. It was as if Mim were hanging my underwear out on the clothesline for everyone to see. Only this time it wasn't on display in the backyard. It was in full view on Main Street.

"Are you okay, Lucy?"

I didn't know what to say. It was strange having someone tell you they'd uncovered your past. I'd been found out. It changed everything. This morning I had left Lila's thinking that I'd stay awhile. But now . . . there was no way it could work. Brian knew and he'd always know.

"You haven't told anyone, have you?" I asked. "Not Lila or Mr. Tariyoko?" He shook his head. "And you didn't contact anyone back in New York to tell them I was here?"

"Lucy, why would I do that?"

"You might feel like it was your responsibility to let people know I was still alive."

"I think that's up to you."

"Please don't tell anyone, Brian."

"Are you in some kind of trouble?"

"No. Not unless my uncles find out I'm still alive. Then I have no idea what might happen."

"Can I ask why you left?"

"It wasn't something I planned. The fire happened. I was ready to go. It's hard to explain. My life wasn't my own back there. I'm not even related to the Sandonis. That's why I came here—to look for my real family."

"Does your family live in Gardenia?"

"I'm not sure."

"Maybe I could help you find them. I know everyone in these parts."

"It's not like that, Brian." I didn't want to explain myself to him.

"What's it like, then?"

"I don't know who they are. I know that sounds strange, but I don't even know their real name. I just know that when I meet them, it'll be right. It'll feel right somehow." Tears began to well up behind my eyes. Brian reached over and put his arm around me, but I pulled away and stood up.

"I know you want me to tell you the whole story,

but I can't, Brian. It's too complicated and you probably wouldn't believe it. I barely believe it myself. Besides, there's a very good chance that I'll be moving on from here."

"Why?"

"If *you* found out, it's only a matter of time until everyone in Gardenia does."

"So what? What do you think will happen if people know your story?"

"They'll never be able to see me for who I really am. I'll forever be Lucretia Sandoni. I'll never escape from that small suffocating self. Can't you see, Brian? I just wanted to have the chance to start over and do it my way this time. But you know about me now. You'll never be able to see me any other way, either."

"Wait a second, Lucy. You think because I know where you come from that I'll feel or treat you differently?"

"Yes!" The pitch of my voice was rising. "You can't pretend that it makes no difference. Won't you always be wondering if I'll change my name and disappear again? Be honest, Brian . . . won't you always be wondering?"

"No. You're the girl I met on the train. Your name is Lucy Buick. You're different now than you were then. And you'll be different next week and the week after. Everyone changes. No one stays the same.

What difference does it make what your name is? What's in a name, anyway?"

"Everything. Everything is in a name. Maybe it's not a big deal to you, because you've always known your real name. You never had to go looking for who you are."

"You make it sound like you're going to find yourself in the next county or the next state. It seems to me that you could look your whole life . . . out there, and never find what you want."

"If I don't look, Brian, I'll never know."

"What if you've already found them, Lucy, but you just can't recognize them? How would you even know?"

"I'll know, Brian. There'll be a sign. I'll feel it."

"And if you don't?"

"I'll find them. I will."

CHAPTER FIFTEEN

"THEY SAID THEY'D STOP BACK LATER TODAY," Lila said. "They didn't leave their names."

She stood over the kitchen sink washing off a bunch of carrots from her garden. She was wearing Jimmy's latest gift on her finger—a big red imitation ruby circled in diamonds. Maybe Lila had decided not to end up a lonely old lady after all.

"What did they look like?" I asked, my heart pounding.

"Well, sort of average in most ways. One was a

little on the tall side. The other had black hair and a longish nose. They looked like insurance salesmen to me." She suddenly reached up to the shelf above the sink and turned up the volume on her little two-way radio. "Wait! I want to hear this."

"The National Weather Service has issued a severe storm warning for Melrose and South Fork counties until late this evening. A high wind advisory is in effect for Suffolk and Windham counties. Stay tuned for updates from the station that gives you more weather on the hour—WDDV, Oskaloosa."

"I've been keeping my eye on that sky all afternoon," Lila said, pointing out the window. "I don't like the look of it and neither does Rufus." Rufus was pacing the kitchen. It looked as if his fever was just about ready to break. "It's too still out there. Eerie, isn't it?"

I looked out to the east. The sky was a slate gray and there was no hint of a breeze. It did look strange. The sky never got that color back in Hamlin. It frightened me, but I didn't have time to think about a storm now. I wanted to know more about these men who were looking for me.

"Did they say anything else, Lila?"

"Who's that, honey?"

“The men who stopped by.” I tried to keep my voice calm, but inside I felt shaky.

“No. They just said they’d catch up with you sooner or later.”

“Frank and Rocco,” I whispered.

“What?”

“Nothing.” Lila had described them perfectly. “What did you tell them?”

“I told them you went to town and I wasn’t sure when you’d be back.” My mind started to race. I couldn’t believe that only two days before, Brian had pulled the newspaper clipping about my death out of his pocket, and now my uncles were here. It was too much of a coincidence. What a fool I’d been. Maybe Lila and Mr. Tariyoko knew the truth as well. And Rhodi. Of course, Rhodi would know. She knew everything. I’d been betrayed. There was no other word to describe what I felt.

I had almost begun to believe that the uncles had forgotten about me and that I was free. But I guess that wasn’t the way it worked in the Sandoni family. It wasn’t in the Sandoni blood to give up.

“I have to go, Lila.”

Lila dried her hands on a towel and came over to me. “Do you know those men, Lucy?” she asked, touching my shoulders. She looked worried. “Are you running from them?”

"I just have to go."

"Now, Lucy, you know I wouldn't pry. It's not my way. But if you're in some kind of trouble, maybe I can help. I've been in a few . . . awkward positions myself in the past."

"Thanks, Lila, but it's not something anyone can help me with. I'll be fine. I just need to keep moving."

Lila eyed me suspiciously. "All I'm saying, honey, is—"

"I appreciate everything, Lila, I do," I interrupted her. "I never should have stayed this long. I'd forgotten what I set out to do. It's time for me to move on." I picked up Rufus and kissed the top of his head, then handed him to Lila. She looked as if she might cry.

"We sure are going to miss you, honey. Isn't that right, Rufus?"

I had to leave then, that instant, before I changed my mind. I couldn't afford to get sidetracked for even a minute longer. I steeled myself and held out my hand to Lila.

"Thank you, Lila, for your hospitality."

Lila wouldn't take my hand. Instead she threw her arms around me, squishing Rufus between the two of us. He let out a squeak.

"Where will you go, Lucy?"

"I'm not sure. Get back on the train, I guess, and keep heading west."

"Will you drop us a line and let us know where you are?"

I nodded, knowing I wouldn't. I couldn't risk having anyone trace me with a postmark or a telephone number. I had to disappear again. Really disappear and never be found.

"Will you tell Yono you're leaving?"

"Yes, I'll pack a few things and see him before I go," I lied again. I walked toward the door, and Lila held it open for me and stuck her head outside.

"Can you at least wait until after this storm passes? I hate to see you go off with bad weather on the way. Storms out here are different than in the East, Lucy. Let me at least take you to the station." She was trying hard not to cry.

I shook my head. "I'll be fine." But inside I was scared. The sky was changing by the minute. The longer I stood there, the greater the possibility that Frank and Rocco would return.

Lila didn't say any more. I knew that she wanted to hug me again and not let me go, and I knew if I let her, I'd have to tell her everything.

"Goodbye, Lila," I said. I turned and walked out the door.

The air was very still and humid and the clouds—all those cumulus clouds Brian had been watching for days—were rising higher in the sky. I went back to my room, gathered my few belongings and wrote a note to Mr. Tariyoko. Lila could read it to him.

> Dear Mr. Tariyoko,
> Glad I had the chance to meet you while I was passing through. I'm on my way somewhere else now. Thanks for trusting me with the monarchs.
> Lucy

I couldn't face him just then. I was afraid he'd tell me something wise and make me change my mind.

The color of the sky had deepened to a dark gray by the time I taped the note to the front of Mr. Tariyoko's door. If I was going to beat this storm and get to the train depot for the 5:45 train, I had better hurry. I walked away from Lila's, keeping my eyes on the eastern sky—the place where the storm was being born. I wished I could be out there right now, a little gust of wind working itself into something big, something that could sweep across hundreds of miles and then change suddenly into a raindrop or a cloud vapor and disappear forever.

I started down the driveway and then turned back. It wasn't safe. If my uncles were driving up the River Road again, they'd be sure to see me. I stared at the cornfield. The corn was well above my head now, but I could see no other way than to cut across the field.

I walked to the edge and looked down a long row. If I just headed west, in the direction of the sun and away from the storm, I would be fine. Even if the skies did open up, I would be safely tucked inside the corn. I wouldn't be alone, either. The wild rabbits would be scrambling through the stalks, headed for the safety of their burrows, and all the cicadas would be taking cover, folding their wings in against the growing wind. A dragonfly blew onto my sleeve, stared at me with its bulbous eyes, flew up under a corn leaf and attached itself there. All creatures were heading for home, and the ones whose homes were too far away were finding the next best thing.

This was the storm Brian had been tracking. He was probably chasing it down. Brian. It was hard for me to even think about him. He'd seemed so sincere . . . so honest. I guess you could never really know a person. Not really.

I had just begun to let myself believe that starting a new life in Gardenia had been the right thing to do. I had even begun to think that Lila and Mr. Tariyoko and Brian had all been worthy signs that I should stay, even if I didn't find the Buicks here. But that wasn't true anymore.

"I'm going to miss this place," I said out loud to the cicadas, trying to hold back my tears as I disappeared into the corn. Even if I'd screamed it, no one would have heard. The insects' song was deafening in the hot, still air. It hadn't been this loud the day I arrived. Time had passed. The cicadas had settled in. They were getting comfortable in the cornfields and along the roadsides. They were getting bold, forgetting they were at the bottom of the food chain. Obviously, they didn't care. They'd find each other, fall in love, lay their eggs and break each other's tiny hearts, if cicadas had hearts—all before the first frost.

"Leave!" I shouted to them. "Leave while you still can." The cicada lovers answered in a wave of defiant buzz. Who was I to give them advice? And what difference did it make, anyway, when your life was only four months long? They might as well go for it. Fall in love, mate and die before they could feel the pain.

I started walking down one row of corn and then another, trying to go in the same westward direction. Occasionally a row would end and I had to walk back and cut across to find another row that was straight. I kept doing this, walking forward, cutting back, cutting across, until I was completely confused. I was beginning to doubt whether the train station was really west of me at all. I didn't even know where west was anymore. The sun was gone, covered by the menacing clouds, and a light rain was beginning to fall. I changed direction, only to change again. Thinking I heard a truck engine backfire, I ran toward the sound. But it wasn't an engine; it was a clap of thunder. I could feel panic rising inside me. Wherever I went I was confronted by another row of corn that looked identical to the last.

A chain of lightning lit the sky, and another clap of thunder echoed around me. I was all turned around, and I was scared. I started running. As I ran, the leaves of corn, those same gentle leaves that held caterpillars and swayed in the evening breeze, whipped against my face, cutting my skin. The wind began to blow through the field, and suddenly there were insects everywhere. In my hair and flying into my eyes. I wanted to scream. I covered my head with my hands and kept running, brushing the insects away from me. I was like a crazy woman, arms flailing around me, barreling headlong into the corn.

Finally, a corn stump stopped me and I tripped and fell on my knees. There was another crack of thunder. I looked up at the sky. It was a strange, dirty green color. A growling sound was coming from somewhere far off in the corn. The wind began to tear at my clothes.

I crawled under the corn and pulled the leaves around me. The skies opened up, and it began to hail.

Not little pieces of hail, but golf-ball-sized hail that pelted the corn and bounced off the leaves covering my head. I wanted to cry out for help, but I knew there was no one out there who was going to save me. I was lost.

It suddenly struck me as I lay beneath the corn that I'd always been running toward something or away from something. I had been looking for a life that wasn't real. Looking for a family that didn't exist. The Buicks weren't here in Gardenia or anywhere else. The truth was that my real family had left me in the backseat of a stranger's car.

"Why!" I screamed at the storm. "Why!" What had been so wrong with me that they hadn't wanted me? My cries blended with the howl of the wind. It was as if it were crying for me and with me and all around me. I laid my face in the mud. It didn't matter now. I would never get out of this field. I could finally let the truth in. It didn't matter if I died out here in the middle of nowhere . . . alone . . . as I had always been.

The storm raged on: the wind, the thunder, the lighting, the hail that turned to torrential rain. I lay there . . . just me. No voices of the Sandonis, uncles or aunts, rang in my ears; no signs appeared; no Lucretia Sandoni; no Lucy Buick. Just me . . . alone.

I was so small, I could barely feel myself. So quiet, I could finally breathe.

"Get up, Lucy," said a voice. I didn't move. Someone was peeling the wet corn leaves off me. "It's safe to come out now. The storm is moving off."

I looked up. Rhodi was standing above me, holding out her hand. I'd always been glad to see Rhodi. She'd been my fairy godmother, my enchanted aunt, my fellow adventurer. But now, all I could see was how she'd tricked me. Strung me along the whole time with false hopes.

"You knew, didn't you Rhodi?" I said, pulling myself to my feet. The rain was now a gentle drizzle.

"What do you mean, dear?"

"You knew there were no Buicks. Didn't you?"

"I knew there was a new life waiting for you."

"Some new life," I said, peeling the cornstalks off my shoulders. "And why didn't you warn me, Rhodi? All along you said not to worry about the uncles. You told me they weren't looking for me."

"They're not."

"Then how do you explain that they're here . . . in Gardenia?"

"But Lucy—"

"No but Lucy, Rhodi. This was your plan all along,

wasn't it? You probably got Brian to conspire with you just like you did with Rufus."

"I didn't have anything to do with that, dear. Brian is in love with you. Of course he'd want to know about you. How could I stop him from finding out? And why would I want to?"

"Well, maybe because it would destroy everything we worked for."

"And what is that?"

"My freedom. He told the uncles. And they've come here to take me back to Hamlin."

"That's not true, dear. Remember, I told you they're not looking for you. You have your freedom. You always did."

"How can you say that?"

"You've always been free, Lucy. Even if the boys came looking for you now, do you think they could drag you to Hamlin against your will and force you to live a life you don't want to live?"

"Yes, sometimes I do."

"Then you haven't learned as much as I thought you had. The boys have no control over you. They never did."

"But all the time and money they spent trying to mold me into something. You don't think they'd want some kind of payback if they knew I was still alive? I don't think you remember clearly what they were like, Rhodi. Maybe being dead has affected your memory."

"Maybe being dead has affected yours, Lucy."

"That's the point, Rhodi. I'm not dead. Not really. You were the one who told me that the only way out of that family was to die."

"Yes. I did say that. And you did die. Lucretia Sandoni died in that fire. The Lucretia who was afraid of her uncles, and pampered by her great-aunts, and didn't trust herself. She died and you went on. You went looking for Lucy Buick."

"Lucy Buick doesn't exist."

"I thought that was who I was talking to."

"It's not that easy, Rhodi."

"It is that easy, dear. You changed your name, but you've changed in other ways, too. You're learning to trust yourself, to follow your own signs."

"It's hard for me to believe that, Rhodi, when I can't even find my way out of a cornfield."

"Believe it. It's true. That's why I'll be leaving you soon."

"What?" I felt my stomach tighten.

"My sisters, too. Though, as usual, they disagree with me. You no longer need to listen to the voices of the dead, dear. The time is rapidly coming for you to dwell entirely among the living."

"What about the uncles, Rhodi?"

"The men who came to Lila's aren't your uncles, dear. That's what I've been trying to tell you."

"Then who are they?"

"You've met them before, at the train depot, I believe. Some kind of religious men."

"The Jehovah's Witnesses?"

"Yes, I think that's right."

I suddenly felt ridiculous. "And Brian?"

"He hasn't told anyone but you. He's a nice young man. You've found more than you think you've found in Gardenia, Lucy. You've followed all the right signs so far and they've brought you here."

"But where am I? I'm more confused now than the night I left Hamlin. I'm entirely lost."

Rhodi chuckled. "Come here, dear." She beckoned to me to bend down close to her face. She unwound a bright blue scarf from her neck and placed it around mine. "I'm going to tell you something, Lucy. And I hope you always remember. You were *wanted*. I wanted you and my sisters wanted you. It's a wonderful thing to be wanted. But you weren't born simply to be wanted, Lucy. You were born for a bigger reason than that. It's time for you to go forward now. You're ready. You're no longer lost."

I reached out and embraced her. "Will I see you again, Rhodi?" I said, tears welling up in my eyes.

"No, Lucy. I imagine the sisters will not let you

leave without some dramatic farewell. But I'm on my way. I've decided on New Delhi. I like their clothes . . . and I want to learn how to make chapati."

"I'll miss you."

She smiled. "Look for me in your dreams, my dear. I will always be there." Then she danced around in the corn and began to fade. "Oh, Lucy . . . what did your friend say . . . that dear little Indonesian man?"

"Japanese man, Rhodi. He's Japanese."

"Oh, yes, that's right. What did he say about cornfields?"

"You have to want to get lost in them. That's the quickest way out."

"Exactly." And then she was gone.

CHAPTER SIXTEEN

GETTING LOST ON PURPOSE IS NOT an easy thing to do. Everything in me wanted to become un-lost and reach the edge of the cornfield as soon as possible. I tried to remember how I'd felt under the corn with the storm raging around me. When I hadn't known anything. When I hadn't known who I was or where I'd been or where I was going. And in this way, I found my way to the edge of the cornfield.

"Over here, Lucretia." Hy was waving to me from a small hill above the field.

"Yoohoo, Lucretia," Olly called.

I walked up to greet my great-aunts.

"Lucretia," Mim said, running up to me.

"We've been looking for you," Vi chimed in. She took out her hankie and wiped my face. "You're a mess."

I looked out over the field. It went on for miles. I could have been lost in there forever.

"Look," said Vi as she pointed to a portion of the field where there had once been corn. A whole section of it was missing, as if a huge hand had reached down from the sky and picked an acre of stalks right out of the middle. "You should have seen that beast," Vi went on, her eyes wide with excitement. "We weren't twenty feet from it . . . and neither were you."

"A twister?" I said. They all nodded solemnly. "It touched down for just a moment," they said.

"We've come to say farewell, Lucretia." Olly wiped her eyes and passed a handkerchief to Hy.

"It is not our decision," Hy added. "Our *other* sister suggested parting. Which is all very well for her—on her way to some jungle all rolled up in a swatch of upholstery fabric."

"It's a sari," I said.

"Well, whatever it is, it's ridiculous. A woman her age . . . really."

Vi, Olly and Mim folded their arms across their chests and nodded in agreement. "We all just can't pop off at a moment's notice and do whatever we want," they said in unison.

"Why not?"

"Well, what about you, Lucretia? What will become of you if we all just vanish?" Vi asked.

"I'll be fine, really," I said. And I knew it. For the first time in my life, I knew it was true. They looked at me curiously. "But maybe Frank and Rocco and Onofrio could use a little help," I suggested.

Mim threw up her hands. "Huh. Those three. Hopeless. It would be a waste of our time. Do you know what they've been doing since you left?"

"No, tell me."

"They've torn down the remains of the factory and they're building a . . . I can't even say it."

"I will then," Olly volunteered. "A burlesque hall. They're building a burlesque hall."

"I think they call it a strip club," said Vi.

"Whatever . . . and they're selling all the burned nylon to some big business in Yonkers."

"You're kidding. They certainly didn't waste any time, did they?"

"Heartless fools," Mim said. "The site of our family business and the scene of your tragic death. Is there no respect?"

"I guess they're not really thinking much about me, then."

Vi shook her head. "Lucretia, they're selfish brutes. I hate to say it, but the day of your memorial service, they signed a contract with Polymer Filaments Inc. to take away the whole stock of melted panty hose and turn them into nylon bristles for paintbrushes."

I laughed. All that worry for nothing.

"Well, I guess if *they* don't need you and *I* don't need you, then it looks to me as if you're free," I said. "There must be something you've always wanted to do for yourselves. Somewhere you've always wanted to go?"

They pondered this for a few minutes.

"Florida," said Vi.

"Bermuda," said Mim.

"Alaska," said Olly.

"Shopping. I want to go shopping," said Hy.

They started arguing and it began to pour again.

"Goodbye," I said as they faded into the corn. "Have fun whatever you do."

"Goodbye, Lucretia," they said, sniffling.

I stooped down to pick up Vi's handkerchief, and when I stood up again they were gone. But someone else was there.

"What are you doing here, Mr. Tariyoko?"

"Walking."

"Walking? In this weather?" He was carrying a large black umbrella, but the rain was drenching him. He motioned for me to join him.

"Let's walk a little, Lucy."

"How did you know where to find me?" I asked as I took shelter under the umbrella.

He smiled. "When I was lost in the sugar field as a young boy, it was monsoon season, the fields were like rivers and my mother went looking for me until she found me. I just kept looking."

"But she was your mother, Mr. Tariyoko . . . and she could *see*."

"She was my family, Lucy."

"Oh." I felt my throat tighten.

"I will tell you something," Mr. Tariyoko said.

As we walked the mile and a half back to Lila's, Mr. Tariyko told me about his life. I had never heard him say more than a few short sentences at one time, but he talked for the full forty minutes it took us to get home.

"When I was a young man," he began, "I moved from the island of Okinawa to Hiroshima, Japan. I was very happy there. I had a wife and a son. As you may know, there was a terrible explosion there." I nodded. I had had no idea that Mr. Tariyoko had lived through the atomic bomb.

"I was coming home from Kyoto when it happened. I never made it home. All the people in my village were killed. All family. All friends. I was not close enough to that explosion to lose my own life, but I lost my sight."

"Oh, Mr. Tariyoko. I'm so sorry."

He patted my hand. "As you may know by now, Lucy, I can see with things other than my eyes. The loss of my sight was small compared to the loss of my family."

"What did you do?"

"I became a wanderer. I went to the mountains. After a long time I came to live with the monks there, who were very kind to me. They called me 'man who survived.' " He ran his finger along the scar on his cheek.

"Is that from the bomb too, Mr. Tariyoko?"

He shook his head. "Like you, Lucy, I spent many years looking for my family. I hoped that one of them had escaped. I saw their ghosts in my dreams, and could not accept that they were gone. Before I came to the monks, I took many foolish risks. I was angry. I fought a man for food once and he cut me." Mr. Tariyoko touched the long scar on his face. "My greatest gift."

"I don't understand?"

"This man, he woke me from my sleep, from my grief, from my rage. Whenever I cried after that, the tears would roll down that crease and land . . . here," he said, placing his hand on his heart. "This is where my family from Hiroshima is."

"Do you miss them still?"

"I will always miss them, but I am no longer looking for them."

I smiled and put my hand on his shoulder. "I think that's a good thing, Mr. Tariyoko, isn't it? No longer looking."

"It makes it easier to see what's inside."

I nodded. The rain was still coming down in buckets, but I was beginning to recognize this part of the cornfield now. We were walking up the back way to Lila's.

"It's nice to come in out of the rain," Mr. Tariyoko said as we approached the door to Lila's kitchen.

"Family is not always what you think it will be, is it, Mr. Tariyoko?"

"Family can be very surprising."

I nodded and kissed him on the cheek. "Thank you."

He gestured toward the door, and I opened it quietly and stepped inside. Brian was on the phone and Lila was pacing the kitchen, and Rufus . . . well . . . Rufus was off in the corner eating an avocado.

CHAPTER SEVENTEEN

"DO YOU EVER GET ONE OF those déjà vu feelings?" I asked.

Brian ran his hand over Cracker Jack's head. "Sometimes," he said.

"My great-aunt Rhodi used to get them all the time. You would have liked Rhodi. She could always tell when a storm was coming, but she never used any instruments."

"Did you inherit any of her abilities?"

"Not about the weather. I wasn't really related to

Rhodi, you know. But I think a few of her gifts rubbed off on me."

I broke off a piece of bread and cut a wedge of cheese. Brian and I were having a picnic dinner in his favorite spot, overlooking the reservoir at sunset. The clouds beyond us were white and fluffy. There hadn't been any storms for almost a month now. It was late August and the evenings were getting cool.

"Too bad. There could be a career for you in meteorology. After all, you're fearless. You run right into storms."

"I don't run into storms, Brian. I run into cornfields during storms."

"Same thing. But you didn't actually run away like you thought you would."

"I almost did."

"What stopped you?"

"When I was lost in the cornfield, I had a chance to think about some things."

"Tornadoes will do that to you," Brian said as if he understood, but I don't think anyone could really understand the past two months of my life. It was going to take me a while to make sense of them myself.

"Close your eyes, Lucy," Brian said suddenly.

"Why?"

"Just close your eyes, and no peeking!"

I did as he asked. I could hear Brian rustling around in his backpack.

"Hold out your hands."

"It's not a snake or anything, is it?"

"Just hold out your hands. No questions." I put my hands out and Brian placed something cool and smooth in them.

"Okay. You can look now."

"Brian!" It was a violin. A beautiful caramel-colored fiddle.

"Do you like it?"

"I love it!" I laid the instrument on my lap and reached over and kissed him. "Where did you find it?"

"Tank helped me. We went to a little store over in Crowley. He said your first gig is coming up next weekend and you broke a string on that old one you've been borrowing. Why don't you play a little something and see how it sounds?"

"With pleasure." I stood up and placed the fiddle under my chin. It fit perfectly. I put the bow on the strings and played a song I'd been working on. There were no lyrics yet, but the melody was sweet and haunting. At the second verse, Brian got to his feet and moved behind me, wrapping his arms around my waist. We danced that way with his face in my hair. As I played, I looked out over the town of Gardenia and thought I could see the outline of Rhodi's face in the clouds—just for a minute, and then it was gone.

"Do you believe in ghosts, Brian?" I asked as I lifted the bow from the strings and turned to face him. He bent down and kissed me.

"I love your hair," he whispered, running his fingers through it.

"You do?"

"I do."

"You believe in ghosts?"

"No, I love your hair."

"But what about ghosts?"

"I don't know—maybe."

"Do you think they could exist?"

"I suppose so. Why?"

"Just wondering."

"Are you seeing ghosts tonight, Lucy?"

"No," I said as I pulled him closer to me. "No ghosts tonight."

CHAPTER EIGHTEEN

I DREAMED OF RHODI LAST NIGHT. She was sitting on top of a Buddhist temple, cooking chapati on the shiny, hot tiles. Her hair was all done up with mangoes and kiwis and white lotus blossoms. She was wearing a magenta sari. She carried a little monkey in the crook of one arm.

"Rhodi!" I called to her. "I'm here, Rhodi!" She blew me a kiss, flipped over a row of the small round breads and whispered something in the monkey's ear.

Then she stood up and walked along the roof of the temple, arms straight out to her sides.

She was chanting something in another language. Repeating the same words over and over. It was hypnotizing. I couldn't pull myself away from the strange melody. And suddenly I knew what she was saying. I could understand the words and she was saying them to me.

"Play me a song, Lucy. Play me a song," her words echoed in my mind. "Play me a lovely song, dear."

I picked up my violin and played a song for Rhodi that night in my dream. And in the months that followed I played for others, too. I played for the dead: for Mim, Hy, Vi, Olly and Lucretia Sandoni.

But mostly, I played for the living. For Lila and Jimmy on their wedding day, and every Thursday night at the South Fork Grange with Tankford Hawling and the Chewy Chickens. I played for my uncles and I played for the Buicks, who were not big-boned people with shiny teeth and deep gravelly voices, after all, but a real family whose names were Fortune, McNeil and Tariyoko.

I played for the last batch of monarch butterflies that emerged from their cocoons one warm morning in late August and flew away.

I played for the cicadas when they stopped singing in early September, their passion finally quenched with the frost.

And I played the day the first snow fell over Gardenia, Iowa, and I was still there.

ABOUT THE AUTHOR

RITA MURPHY lives in northern Vermont with her husband and son. Her previous novels are *Harmony*, *Black Angels* and *Night Flying*.